CHALLENGE OF THE RED UNICORN

JACK SCOLTOCK

Jack Scoltock   *Sept 2009*

A VIRTUAL TALES BOOK

Challenge of the Red Unicorn

Cover Art © 2009 Justine Scoltock

Edited by Jake George (www.sagewordsservices.com)
           Sheri Gormley (www.sherigormley.com)

A Virtual Tales Book
PO Box 822674
Vancouver, WA 98682 USA

www.VirtualTales.com

ISBN 1-935460-03-X

First Edition: September 2009

Printed in the United States of America

9 7 8 1 9 3 5 4 6 0 0 3 9

FOR URSULA

WITHOUT YOU I WOULD BE LOST

ALSO AVAILABLE FROM JACK SCOLTOCK

BADGER, BEANO & THE MAGIC MUSHROOM
THE SAND CLOCKER
JUSTINE'S SECRET CHALLENGE
JEREMY'S ADVENTURES
IN THE SHADOW OF THE OAK

COMING SOON FROM JACK SCOLTOCK

THE MELTIN' POT
FROM WRECK TO RESCUE AND RECOVERY

FIRST COMMUNION:
A COLLECTION OF MODERN IRISH STORIES

WWW.JACKSCOLTOCK.COM

CONTENTS

CHAPTER ONE

THE UNICORNS

THE WHITE UNICORNS NEAR THE TREES SHIVERED, their clear black eyes widening as they looked around. They felt uneasy, though they could neither see nor smell the danger... yet.

Raggadan valley, right away down to the tall oak trees where the forest began, was overrun with the beautiful horned creatures. There were thousands of them.

It was a bright night, with a looming green moon lighting up the whole countryside. The unicorns were feeding on the succulent sweet-tasting Shulic—a red, thick-leaved grass which grew in abundance in that part of the land and was especially fertile in the Resting Valley.

Near the top of the valley, a tiny elf uniherd sat on a mound of mossy grass playing softly on his reed pipe. The uniherd occasionally scanned the herd. Always alert, even as he played, he sensed their restlessness, but he could see nothing that endangered them. His pointed ears moved in time to his haunting, beautiful music. The sound of the melodies he played drifted down among the unicorns, but did little to quell the restlessness of those near the forest.

Suddenly several of the oldest creatures whinnied. The sound alerted the uniherd. As he jumped to his feet, he scanned the edge of the herd. Some of the unicorns were huddled in the shadow of the trees. They were standing so still that the uniherd knew they were frightened. All of a sudden the unicorns began to neigh loudly. Those near the trees panicked and tried to run up the valley. Squealing, some of them rose on their hind legs, magic fizzling from their horns like tiny lightning bolts.

In the moonlight the uniherd blinked several times as he tried to see what had frightened them. Then... "Weers!" he gasped when he saw two crouched shapes slip into the meadow from the shadows. Already the beasts had cut off some of the herd and were driving them into the trees. Immediately the uniherd dove for a silver horn that every watcher of the herd carried and blew it hard, but it was already too late. The Weers had disappeared with a small group of about thirty unicorns. As he made his way down through the rest of them, the uniherd worried. He knew help would come, too late. The Weers were too crafty to be caught now.

A minute after the warning sound of the uniherd's horn had echoed down to Derrylyn village, over one hundred heavily armed elves were making their way to the valley, riding bareback on small creatures that resembled Pit Pony horses.

"They were so quick," cried the uniherd. Tears were running down his pale face. "They came out of the trees, there." He pointed to the shadows in the oaks. "They took about thirty away. I'll know the exact number when I count the rest of the head."

Turning to the soldier elves, their General shouted, "Command One, get down to the forest! Search, but be alert and stay together!" He glared after them as fifty of his bravest soldiers raced to the trees.

"The Weers have never come into the Raggadan before," whispered a tall, thin-faced elf called Drollo, who was the General's second in command.

"No," said Gando, General of all the elves. He was a heavily muscled elf of three hundred and eight years. He stood about five feet tall and wore a silver eye patch over one eye.

Gando was dressed in a long, sheepskin-type coat. His hair was long and the grey flecks in it glittered in the moonlight. Around his waist he wore a thick leather belt that hung loose on his wide stomach. A scabbard that held his broadsword was attached to the belt. Gando also had two small, curved daggers sitting snugly in sheaths on both of his upper arms.

The General's ears were broader, though not as pointed as the other elves standing around him. His eyes glowed with power, as all the elves had a little magic. Now Gando turned to the other fifty. "Command Two. Check the perimeter of the valley. If any Weers are seen, do *not* engage with them. Send for me. Now go!" he shouted.

In just a few moments only Gando, the uniherd, and Drollo stood studying the frightened, restless unicorns.

"How many were there in the herd?" Gando asked, turning to the uniherd.

"Eight thousand and forty six, General," replied the still tearful uniherd.

Gando sighed heavily. *It will be a long night*, he thought, hoping with all his heart that what he feared had not happened. "Come," he said to the uniherd. "Accompany Drollo and myself. I must examine every unicorn tonight."

The uniherd frowned as though puzzled. He looked at Drollo. Drollo shook his head at him silently, telling him not to question Gando's reason for the examination... though he wondered about it himself.

It was an hour after Eglin's three suns had risen above Pragg Mountains before Gando had examined almost all the unicorns. His heart was pounding as he came to the last few creatures, but he knew that his greatest fear was true. He had felt it all along. *It's gone*, he thought, a feeling of great dread almost overpowering him. Turning to the uniherd, he murmured quietly, "I'll send forty soldiers to help you guard the herd tonight." He studied the young uniherd's sad face. "Do not reproach yourself, Baggo. You are not to blame."

As Baggo watched Gando and Drollo head back to the village, tears tumbled down his face. He had been dishonored. Twenty-nine unicorns had been stolen. *It was my fault*, he thought. *The General has been kind, but it was my fault. I was not alert enough.*

As they rode into the village Gando said, "Drollo, I want you to come with me to the House of Wisdom. I have to speak urgently with the Wiselfs."

Drollo studied his General's worried face. "What is it, Gando?" he asked. "What has happened?" He knew the theft of the twenty-nine unicorns was worrying, but there was something else that had disturbed Gando.

Gando sighed heavily then said, "It wasn't there, Drollo."

Drollo's frown asked the question.

"The supreme unicorn," said Gando, his mouth suddenly so dry he could hardly say the words. Drollo's gasp made him turn to him. "Yes, Drollo, Chalice," said Gando. "Only I and the Wiselfs knew it was among the main herd."

"But why did they allow Chalice to mingle with the herd? Why didn't they allow it to stay in the garden of Aroon with its mother?" asked Drollo.

"Because the wisdom of the Wiselfs believed it was better for Chalice to be with the older unicorns. They believed Chalice's magic would grow much quicker living among the main herd," answered Gando.

"But Chalice would have stood out among the other unicorns," exclaimed Drollo. "His color would have betrayed him."

"He was disguised. The Wiselfs used a secret dye to color him white," said Gando quietly.

CHAPTER TWO

The Garden of Aroon

The village that Gando and Drollo were hurrying through was about five miles square and was bordered by tall elm and oak trees. In the very center was a cottage that was a hundred times bigger than the thousands of tiny cottages that made up Derrylyn.

Moving quicker now through the narrow cobbled streets, the two elves stopped at a tiny wooden gate that led to the door of the big cottage known as the House of Wisdom. Four elf guards stood outside. They saluted quickly and allowed Gando and Drollo to enter.

Inside, an old elf showed Gando and Drollo to a large room where eight older elves were sitting. Three of them were reading from books with pages made of stiff parchment. Four others were practicing mind games. One elf—the oldest of the group—sat at an oak table that was also crowded with pieces of parchment. He was deciphering an ancient scroll, but he looked up from his studies when Gando and Drollo were shown into the room.

Most of the Wiselfs had silver hair and short beards. They wore black habits and glowed with a magic that showed they were much more powerful than Gando or the other elves.

Drollo felt his heartbeat pound against his chest as he listened to Gando break the terrible news to the Wiselfs.

An hour later three of the oldest Wiselfs hurried quickly through the garden of Aroon towards a beautiful red unicorn and five of her children, who lay feeding on bales of red Shulic at the entrance to a grove of tall pine trees.

The garden of Aroon was about as large as four football stadiums. It was covered in the most brightly colored flowers and fruit trees that bordered a maze of white sandy paths that ran throughout the garden. The bees, birds, and butterflies—colored like no other small creatures—all added to the peacefulness of the beautiful Aroon. The sweet scent of the flowers was everywhere.

As soon as the elves approached the middle of the winding path that led to the grove, the red unicorn whispered to her young ones. "Go down to the fruit trees and finish your feeding. I must speak with our keepers." Whinnying loudly, the young unicorns began to gallop down the path. When they reached the old elves they stopped, whinnied and then reared above them for a few seconds before continuing on down.

Their mother studied the elves when they stopped in front of her. The red hairs on her mane were standing almost straight up as she sensed why they had come.

"You promised me that Chalice would be safe with the herd. You promised me!" she cried in a high-pitched voice.

The elves, realizing she knew about her son, looked uncomfortable. The oldest of them, whose name was Trigon, took two steps towards her and stopped just below the beautiful creature's bowed head. A slight shimmering of magical mist covered the red unicorn's horn completely.

"Yes, Lela," he said quietly, raising his right hand to stroke her horn. "We did promise you. But how could we know the Weers would come this far? They have never come into our part of the land before. They have never come near Raggadan before! But do not worry. The Weers do not know who it is they have taken. Chalice's disguise will fool them."

Lela snickered softly and looked away, but a silver tear slipped down her long nose.

"If they did know," continued Trigon, "you would have felt his..." He stopped, unable to say it.

"His death," whispered Lela as another tear rolled from her left eye. "He may as well be dead. I will never see him again. The Weers will soon find out Chalice is with those who have been taken. Rashark will soon know. Chalice's magic will eventually give him away." Suddenly Lela stamped her feet and swung her head away from the Wiself. "You know if Chalice looses his magic he will die. If he does, all unicorns will die. The land cannot survive without our magic. The evil Rashark will rule. You know what that means?"

Trigon nodded, as did his two companions.

"Chalice will have to be rescued," said Lela neighing loudly.

At the trees her children stopped eating when they heard their mother's worried neigh. They, too, could sense something was wrong. But feeling secure that she was there and that they were safe in the garden, they resumed feeding.

"Rescued? But...?" began Trigon. "There are thousands of the Weer beasts, far too many for us to battle. Rashark's powerful magic would wipe us out if we were to enter his domain."

"His magic will wipe you out anyway if he discovers Chalice," cried Lela, turning to watch her children again.

"What can we do?" asked one of the other Wiselfs.

"There's nothing we can do," said the elf beside him.

Lela whinnied angrily. "There is something you can do," she snapped looking steadily at Trigon.

"What do you mean?" he asked.

"Someone from another land must help us, someone with magic strong enough to face and destroy Rashark and bring Chalice home to the garden."

"But who is this... this someone?" asked Trigon.

"Someone who is good, someone whose magic will get stronger when they enter our land," replied Lela.

Trigon frowned. "Lela. Again I ask you, who?"

The beautiful unicorn whinnied. Then she said two words that had the three old elves gasping.

"Human Kind."

Trigon was the first to speak. "Hu... Human Kind?" He gulped.

"Yes," said Lela turning to watch two of her children begin a playful fencing game with their horns. "A young Human Kind."

"But... but we cannot allow a Human Kind to enter our land!" exclaimed one of the other Wiselfs. "You know that the way here—through the Warke tunnel—is always guarded by a thousand of our strongest elves in case anyone from another land should try to enter. No Human Kind would ever be allowed to enter our land. They would be killed at once. Those are General Gando's orders."

Lela whinnied loudly, this time her nostrils flared slightly as she thought about the Warke, the mysterious winding tunnel that led to and from other lands. Then she said quietly, "My son must be rescued. If Chalice dies, then all the land will die. Chalice must be rescued. His magic must be allowed to grow."

The three elves looked at each other.

"But a Human Kind?" said Trigon. "Is there no other way?"

Lela neighed angrily, rising suddenly on her hind legs. As she pawed at the air above Trigon's head she screamed, "There *is* no other way! There is no one in our land who can save my son! You have to bring a Human Kind here to save him! You must go to the ancient Oracle. Ask the Oracle to show you the Human Kind who would be the most suitable. The Oracle will show you. Now go!"

Then Lela swung away and galloped down to her children.

The elves studied the unicorns for several seconds then hurried to the exit from the garden. They were all deeply distressed. *A Human Kind,* each thought silently to himself.

꧁❦꧂

When the elves had gone and her children were sleeping, Lela thought now about the wisest of the elves, Dardo. *I wish he had been here. Dardo would have known what to do.* She wished now she was allowed to leave the garden, but she had her other children to consider. Besides, what good would she be anyway? She couldn't face Rashark.

A single tear slipped down her beautiful face, glistening like a diamond as it tumbled to the ground. "Chalice. Oh my Chalice where are you?"

CHAPTER THREE

THE ORACLE

IN A CAVERN THE SIZE OF A CATHEDRAL, THE EIGHT Wiselfs stood about ten meters back from a clear pool of water. The light inside the cavern was a dull blue color, as was the water. The walls were as smooth as polished marble, and glowing obelisks—each three meters tall— protruded from the floor. Ancient elfin words were cut into each of them, and the whole cavern hummed with powerful magic.

Trigon moved away from the others carrying a curved uniherd's staff that had a unicorn's head carved on the top end of it and stopped right at the very edge of the pool. As the other Wiselfs held their breath, he stamped with the end of the staff on a block of black crystal that jutted out of the water. The dull thud of the staff as it hit the crystal was almost immediately followed by a spark of light that shot out from it, arcing into the pool. As the light fizzled into the water, a low hiss echoed around the cavern.

The seven Wiselfs moved closer to each other now as the water began to bubble and boil, and a mist quickly began to form on top of the water. When the mist became thick and white, the bubbling subsided.

"Oracle!" shouted Trigon, who still stood on the edge of the pool. "We need your wise counsel! We ask you to use your ancient knowledge to help us in this—our most urgent need!" Trigon stamped the staff against the black crystal again. As another magical spark hissed into the water, the mist grew even thicker, forming a cloud about three meters high that floated over the pool. It was so thick that none of the Wiselfs could see the water.

Suddenly a voice began speaking, and even though the Wiselfs had heard this voice before, their skin tingled and their hair creeped along the back of their necks from fear.

"Why do you disturb my slumber?" the voice boomed from the head of a black unicorn that now appeared above the mist. "Why have you summoned the Oracle who sees all?" The Oracle's glowing red eyes glared at Trigon.

"We need your help with a matter that must be resolved, or our land will perish!" shouted Trigon.

"A matter?" boomed the voice.

"Chalice!" shouted Trigon. "The supreme unicorn has been taken by the Weer beasts. The magical son of the great Lela is in danger. He must be saved!"

"Why do you come to me with this? The unicorn Queen Lela has the wisdom that could advise you," boomed the Oracle.

"She has advised us," said Trigon. "She told us that only a Human Kind can save Chalice. Only a Human Kind would have the power to face Rashark." Trigon paused then added, "A Human Kind has never been allowed to enter our land before."

The Oracle turned its head slightly and then said, "There is always a first time."

"Then... then you agree with Lela? A Human Kind must be brought through the Warke?" asked Trigon.

The Oracle turned his head slightly left and then right, and said, "You wish to see the Human Kind who will help you?"

Trigon turned back to look at the others, and they nodded. Turning back to the Oracle he said, "There are many Human Kind, many more than the million elves and creatures who live in Eglin. Yes, Oracle, we would like to see this special Human Kind."

The Oracle's head descended into the mist, and a scene appeared where its head had been. It showed a small boy with reddish-blond hair and bright green eyes. He wore a tee-shirt, blue jeans and running shoes. He was walking along a country road.

"His name is Eoin. You will find him in a place called Ireland. He lives with other children in the town of Cloonalagh. He is the only Human Kind boy who has magic. His magic will grow a thousand fold when he enters this land through the Warke."

The scene vanished as quickly as it came. "Go now and leave me to sleep. You have disturbed me."

The mist suddenly disappeared, and as the Wiselfs turned to leave the pool grew calm again.

Outside the cavern, at the foot of a low hill where thick bushes grew, the Wiselfs discussed the Oracle's words. The youngest of the Wiselfs, who was four hundred and eight years old asked, "Who will go through the Warke to this Ireland and bring the Human Kind through it?"

The Wiselfs looked at each other. Then Trigon said, "I will go and I will take General Gando with me."

The others stared at him, not envying him the task of entering the mysterious Warke. "Come," said Trigon. "There is little time to waste. We must make plans. We must exercise all of our magical concentration to get Gando and myself to this land called Ireland. Do not forget that only one has entered the Warke to leave our land before—and he has yet to return."

As the Wiselfs hurried back to the village, Trigon thought about Dardo. There was no Wiself like him, and he remembered the night that Dardo had disappeared. The soldiers guarding the Warke had not even tried to stop him; Dardo just pushed past them and leapt into it, saying only, "I will return." That had been over two years ago. Since then, a law had been passed that no one was allowed to enter the Warke without the permission of all the Wiselfs.

Later the Wiselfs sat around the great oak council table, waiting for the General to arrive.

"If you enter the Warke you will never return!" exclaimed one Wiself.

"How do you know you will arrive in the right land—this... Ireland?" asked another.

Gando entered the room and took a seat at the council table with a frown. *Enter the Warke? What is this all about?* he thought.

It was then Trigon stood up. Addressing Gando he said, "I'm sure you are puzzled by what we have been saying. It has been decided that you will accompany me into the Warke."

Gando's eyes widened at the words, but he said nothing.

Trigon explained to him. "Gando, Lela has told us there is only one who can help us save Chalice. The Oracle has shown us where the Human Kind lives."

"A what? A Human Kind?" Gando looked around the other Wiselfs. They nodded.

"Yes. A boy Human Kind," said Trigon. "You and I are going to enter the Warke, go to his land and bring him back with us."

"But Trigon, again I ask you—how do you know you will arrive in the right land?" asked the Wiself who had spoken before.

"By using all our combined magic and concentration," answered Trigon. "We must use our magic in a way we have never before," he said moving away from the table. "Come, we have little time to waste."

Shortly a thousand guards that where lined up in front of the Warke were moving aside to allow the Wiselfs to approach the entrance.

Gando, who was the bravest of all the elves, gulped as he stared into the cave. The Warke was inside it, and already he could hear the roar as it waited. Above the entrance to the cave written in ancient elfin were the words, *The way to and from many lands.*

"Come, Gando," said Trigon. "Let us enter the Warke." He looked at the other Wiselfs. Already they had their eyes closed and were standing in a circle, holding onto each others hands. Magic was beginning to flash around and around them. Occasionally some of it shot into the cave seeking the way into the Warke.

A few seconds later, Gando and Trigon were standing right at the edge of the swirling, sucking black tunnel that was the Warke. Already they could feel the pull of the Warke as Trigon's habit billowed out towards it. Both of them could feel the magic swirling around them from the other Wiselfs.

"Gando!" shouted Trigon above the roar. "Hold my hand! Quickly! We do not want to be separ—"

Gando was just in time to grab the Wiself's hand when they where both suddenly sucked forward into the Warke. The magic from the Wiselfs outside surrounded Trigon and Gando protectively as their minds, unable to stand the babble of strange voices, the fierce buffeting and speed with which they shot through the Warke, lost consciousness.

CHAPTER FOUR

Human Kind

Eoin knocked on the bottom half of the cottage door.

"There's no need to knock, Eoin," said a quiet voice.

Eoin smiled excitedly as he entered the sweet-smelling interior of the cottage. The tiny, thatched and whitewashed building was situated about half a mile outside Cloonalagh, and about thirty meters from the entrance to a long lane that led down to the river Cloon. Only fishermen frequented this lane during the fishing season.

"What are we going to do today, Arthur?" Eoin asked the white-haired old man who was sitting at a table, reading a thick, leather-bound book.

Arthur was smaller than Eoin, and his hair was almost shoulder length. He wore a battered corduroy cap. Eoin had never seen the old man bare-headed.

"Today we are going down to the river. I want to show you something that you will enjoy doing all your life," said Arthur.

Eoin waited impatiently at the door as Arthur rose from the table and then reached for his tattered tweed coat that had leather patches on the elbows. Smiling,

Arthur gently pushed Eoin out of the door in front of him. They had only gone a few meters when Arthur turned and pointed at the door. Eoin smiled when he saw the door close and he heard the bolt inside slip into place.

Just as Arthur turned and pulled on his coat, a tiny bird, a tomtit flew from a low bush in the garden and landed on his shoulder. The old man frowned when he saw a thick elastic band was caught in the poor creature's beak.

"Ah, you poor, wee thing," he whispered reaching to lift the bird into his wizened hands. In a few seconds he had freed the bird. As it flew around Arthur's shoulders, the elastic band fell to the ground. Eoin picked it up and put it into his pocket.

"Come on, Eoin," said Arthur. "Today might be the day."

"What day?" asked Eoin hurrying to keep up with the old man.

"You'll find out," said Arthur a twinkle in his deep green eyes.

As Eoin hurried down the lane, more birds landed on Arthur's shoulders. One cheeky sparrow even landed on top of the old man's cap. All of the birds were whistling happily. They were obviously unafraid of Arthur.

About halfway down the lane, they came to a huge log that blocked their way. Suddenly, with a loud whoop, Arthur leapt over it, clearing the log by a good meter.

Smiling, Eoin shook his head then leapt over the log, too. His right heel caught the top of it, though he landed safely on the other side. As he caught up with Arthur, a thought came to him about how agile the old man was. "Arthur, what age are you?"

Arthur stopped. With a huge grin he said, "That's not very polite, asking someone their age, but what age do you think I am?"

Eoin studied his pink wrinkled face. "I don't know, about sixty-seven?"

"Hah!" laughed Arthur. "What if I was to tell you I am six hundred and fourteen years old? Would you believe me?"

Eoin frowned. "Six hundred and fourteen years old? No, I wouldn't believe you... but you've never lied to me before, have you?"

Arthur's eyes widened. "What do *you* think?" he asked, smiling. Before Eoin could answer him the old man said, "Come on, we don't want to be late."

Suddenly a rabbit hopped out of the hedge and Arthur bent over to pick it up. Stroking it gently, he led the way on down the lane. As they headed to the river Eoin thought about the first time he had met Arthur.

⚜

Cloonalagh Orphanage, where Eoin lived with twenty-eight other boys and twenty-two girls, was a red bricked Victorian building, situated right on the edge of town. The orphanage was adjacent to Cloonalagh School. Sister Attracta, who was the kindest of the five nuns who looked after the children, often wondered who

Eoin's mother was, and why had she given up her beautiful baby.

The kind nun loved Eoin as if he were her own child. She knew him to be kind and thoughtful, yet he never seemed to enjoy the company of other children. He preferred to be on his own. Eoin always appeared sad and thoughtful, yet these past few months she noticed that he seemed to be much happier. It was good that he was happy.

During the summer holidays, Eoin would often go for long walks out into the countryside. He loved the quietness of the country and enjoyed watching the wild creatures that were abundant in that part of Ireland. It was on one of those days that he first met Arthur. He had often passed the old derelict cottage, but this day he noticed smoke coming from the chimney. *Someone must be living there now*, he thought looking at the open half-door. The gate in front of the short path leading to the cottage was broken and lay at an angle, allowing the curious boy to slip up the path. He edged towards the door and peered over the lower half of the door into the semi-darkness. By the fireplace he saw Arthur, who had his back to him.

Without turning Arthur had said, "Don't be standing there gawking. Come on in."

Arthur's voice had sounded so kind and gentle that Eoin unbolted the lower half of the door and stepped inside. That day he stayed, helping Arthur clean out the old cottage until it was almost dark. The first thing—the first magical thing—had happened that very evening. One of the panes in the window was cracked, and Eoin had mentioned to Arthur as he cleaned the other pane that it would have to be replaced. But the old man simply smiled and spoke in a voice that Eoin had grown to recognize meant that something strange was going to happen.

"Come here and watch! I am going to show you something, and when I teach you how to do it I want you to promise me you'll never show anyone else."

Puzzled, Eoin had watched as Arthur ran his forefinger along the crack in the glass. Suddenly, something happened that had Eoin's eyes wide with wonder. A blue, glowing light had fizzled from Arthur's finger and along the jagged crack in the pane.

"Have a look now," said Arthur, smiling.

Eoin had studied the glass. There was no sign of the crack. But the next words that Arthur spoke were even more amazing... and they had made Eoin return almost every day since.

"I'll teach you how to do that," Arthur told him softly, with a quick wink of his eye. And true to his word, he had—along with other things that Eoin would not have thought possible.

Later, when he got to know Arthur better, Eoin told the old man how he had come to live in the orphanage. Sister Attracta—his favorite nun—had found him lying in front of the big oak door of the orphanage one winter's night. He was wrapped in a blue blanket, and around his neck there was a silver chain and a silver holy medal, which he wore even to this day.

They reached the river a half-minute later.

"We'll head up past the Carrie," said Arthur. "There's a place there that should be suitable."

Wondering what they were going to do, Eoin followed Arthur. The Carrie was a small waterfall that allowed the salmon and trout to get to the upper reaches of the river. The calm water above the falls was alive with flies and other insects. Occasionally, a splash and the ripples that eddied onto the river bank told Arthur and Eoin that a fish had taken an insect.

Soon they came to a niche cut out of the bank by numerous floods, and jumping down onto the sandy bottom, Arthur looked around.

Frowning, Eoin did the same. Eoin could feel his excitement increasing as he wondered what magic Arthur was going to show him today.

"Now," said Arthur, looking around again. "Watch." Bending, the old man placed the tip of his forefinger into the water. Mumbling words that Eoin could now understand, Arthur closed his eyes and almost immediately, blue magic poured from his forefinger into the water. Seconds later, he opened his eyes and turned to study Eoin. "You heard the words?"

Eoin nodded. He looked at the water, wondering what was going to happen.

"You remember them?" asked Arthur, his eyes now fixed on the water.

"Yes."

Eoin almost fell into the water when a huge salmon stuck its shiny, pointed head out and stared at them with glistening eyes. Then another salmon appeared, then two trout. A long eel as thick as a man's arm began to wriggle about, occasionally lifting its head out of the water to stare at them. Within seconds there were over a hundred fish looking at Arthur and Eoin. Some of them were beginning to leap about.

Unexpectedly, Arthur snapped his fingers and within two seconds, the fish disappeared below. The water became calm again.

"Now it is your turn, Eoin," said Arthur.

Eagerly, Eoin bent down over the water. Putting his right forefinger into it, he said the words he had heard Arthur say. Closing his eyes, he concentrated the way Arthur had taught him. Slowly at first, the magic began to seep from his finger, then it grew faster.

While Eoin was concentrating, Arthur was staring up the riverbank. He frowned when he saw movement. Someone was coming.

Seconds later Eoin opened his eyes. Grinning, he saw the fish begin to appear. "I've done it, Arth—," he said as he looked around, but Arthur was gone.

"Arthur?" he shouted.

Suddenly, he gave a start when he looked up the bank. Two strange looking people were running towards him. Remembering the fish, he snapped his fingers and immediately they disappeared. He looked again for Arthur, but he was nowhere to be seen.

Now rising to his feet, Eoin saw the strangers had pointed ears. Frightened, he scrambled up onto the bank and got ready to run. He was still wondering where

Arthur had gone and was turning to run when a voice stopped him.

"Eoin."

One of the strange men had called his name. Turning, but still ready to run, Eoin asked, "How do you know my name? Who are you?"

"Human Kind," said Gando coldly. "We need your help."

Eoin studied the strange looking little man who was almost as big as he was. "My... my help?" he stammered, wondering what this was all about.

"Yes. You will come with us," said Gando.

But backing away Eoin shouted, "I'm coming with no one!" He looked around. "Arthur!" he yelled, and suddenly he had turned and was racing away. But he had only gone a few steps when Trigon pointed at him. A blue spurt of magic hit Eoin on the back of the head, and with a soft sigh he tumbled to the ground.

In a few moments Gando and Trigon were standing over him.

"How is this Human Kind ever going to save Chalice?" asked Gando. "He can't even save himself."

"The Oracle has said that he is the one," said Trigon. "Bring him. We must hurry back to the Warke. We do not have much time."

CHAPTER FIVE

Eoin Meets Lela

From his hiding place in thick bushes, Arthur watched as Trigon and Gando carried Eoin back the way they had come. Silently, the old man hurried after them. He was just in time to see the elves push through some bushes near a group of chestnut trees. When they were out of sight, he began to slip closer.

They were standing between some huge, lichen-covered boulders that had thick, thorny whin bushes growing all around them. Trigon muttered a few ancient elfin words as he waved his hands in front of his body. The roar as the Warke appeared was deafening and right away the two elves felt their long hair whipping around their faces as it pulled at them.

Suddenly Trigon saw Gando pull his sword from its sheath. Holding Eoin with one hand, he looked around.

Arthur, who was watching, froze.

"What is it, Gando?"

"I… I don't know. I feel we're being watched."

"No matter," said Trigon, looking at the Warke. He was anxious to get back. "We must go now."

Frowning, Gando looked around again. Slowly sheathing his sword, he gripped Eoin tighter. The Warke sucked harder at the two elves and the Irish boy as they edged closer. As they did, Trigon reached out to grip Gando's belt and suddenly the pull of the Warke was too strong. They were sucked inside and were whirling through it. The powerful magic of the seven Wiselfs was drawing them back to Eglin even as they lost consciousness.

Meanwhile, the instant Arthur saw Trigon, Gando and Eoin disappear into the Warke, he came out of hiding. Alarmed, he saw the entrance to the Warke was disappearing. Immediately he began to race towards it. But as he did, he failed to see a short, round piece of branch lying on the ground, and before he could stop himself his feet were in the air and he was falling with a thud onto his back.

Dazed, he scrambled to his feet, but when he looked for the entrance to the Warke, it was gone. Panicked now, he waved his hands, screaming several ancient spells. *Where is it?* he thought. It was just then that the misty outline of the Warke entrance reappeared. Arthur screamed again and then leapt forward, disappearing into it. But it was only a few seconds later as he was traveling through the Warke that he realized that he was too late.

❧

It seemed like only seconds had passed, but it was over an hour later when the seven Wiselfs saw Trigon and Gando carrying a quickly recovering Eoin come out of the cave. Everyone including the guards gathered around them. The elves studied the strange boy as Gando gently lowered him to the mossy ground. Then straightening, he shouted to the guards. "Get to your positions and be alert! We might have been followed."

Just then Eoin gave a groan. "Whe... where am I?" he asked, sitting up and looking around. He gaped at the strange little men standing before him.

"Do not be afraid, Human Kind," said Trigon quietly, realizing Eoin would be afraid.

But bending over, Gando pulled Eoin roughly to his feet. With a cry of both anger and fear, Eoin pulled away from him. In doing so, he almost tripped over one of the Wiselfs who was standing behind him.

"Where am I?" he repeated. "Where's Arthur?" Eoin's eyes widened as he looked around again. *Where am I?* he thought.

"We know of no Arthur," said Trigon. "You were alone when we came for you."

Eoin studied the little men. "Who or what are you? Is there a circus in town?" Eoin and several of the children had been to a circus last year with Sister Attracta. It had been one of the most enjoyable days of his life.

"The Human Kind is frightened and confused," Gando said to Trigon, wondering how this boy, this Human Kind, was going to rescue Chalice.

"Yes," said Trigon. "It's understandable, I suppose." To Eoin he said, "Human Kind, if you come with us to the garden of Aroon, we will try to answer all of your questions. We would like you to meet Lela."

Though still angry and a little frightened, Eoin snapped as he backed away from Trigon, "I'm not going anywhere until you tell me where I am." He was still wondering where he was and who the strange little men were. Something wasn't right. "You'd better answer me or I'll tell the Police."

"The Police?" The big General looked at Trigon.

"We do not know of whom you speak," said the old Wiself. "Look, Human Kind—"

"Why do you keep calling me that?" asked Eoin.

"What?" said Trigon.

"Human Kind?"

"You are one, aren't you?" growled Gando.

"What?" said Eoin, all the while thinking, *I'm in an insane asylum or somewhere worse.*

"A Human Kind," said Trigon. "Look, we really do not wish you harm. Quite the contrary, we need you to help save our land."

Eoin frowned. "Save? Save your land? What do you mean?"

"Come," said Trigon reaching out to touch Eoin gently on the shoulder. With an angry snort, Eoin pulled away from him.

At this Gando growled. He was growing impatient with Eoin.

"Please, Human Kind," said Trigon quietly. "We will not harm you. We cannot harm you. You are our only hope."

Eoin studied the old elf, then he looked at Gando and the other elves, then he looked around again. Nothing seemed familiar. He didn't know where he was. There was no direction he could run. He looked over at the guards who were standing around the cave. "What's in there?" he asked.

Trigon's answer shocked him.

"That is the Warke. It's the way back to your land. But you will never be able to return unless we use our magic to direct you there. Human Kind, I promise that when you have saved our land, we will return you safely to yours."

Gando shook his head as he studied Eoin. *Save our land*, he thought. *This boy? Huh. This little Human Kind?* He sighed. *It's been a waste of time. How will this boy, even if he is a Human Kind, have any hope of overpowering Rashark?*

"What do you mean, to mine?" asked Eoin. "Are you trying to tell me I'm not in Cloonalagh?" He looked around again. It was when he looked up that he saw it was true. He gaped at Eglin's three suns, and he knew instantly he was not even in Ireland. "Where the heck am I?" he gasped.

"In Eglin," said Trigon. "Human Kind, please come with us to the garden. You can speak with Lela. She will explain how you are to rescue her son."

"Rescue her son?" exclaimed Eoin. "What are you talking about? Look, are you sure you have the right person?"

"Eoin, point your right forefinger up at the sky," Trigon said patiently.

Eoin frowned at the old Wiself's strange request. Gando was frowning, too. *What is this?* he thought.

"What did you say?" said Eoin.

"Point your right forefinger upwards," said Trigon.

"Do it, Human Kind," snapped Gando, his impatience showing.

Puzzled, Eoin pointed upwards.

"Now," said Trigon. "Look at the tip of your finger, then look up."

Frowning, Eoin looked at the tip of his finger, and then up at the clear blue sky with its three suns. Suddenly, magic hummed all around him and fizzling, lightning-like sparks swirled up his body and into his arm. Just when he thought his arm was going to be torn from his body, the pressure was instantly relieved as a blast of blue magic erupted from his finger. The shock of the powerful blast threw him backwards into the other Wiselfs.

Equally shocked, Gando gaped at Eoin. Magic still spluttered from Eoin's finger.

The General smiled as he looked around the other elves. They were all staring, astonished at Eoin's power. *We might have a chance after all*, thought Gando as he reached down to help Eoin to his feet.

"How... how on earth did that happen?" asked Eoin looking at his finger that still spluttered with magic. "It was never as powerful as *that* before."

"It's the magic," said Trigon. "Your magic is greater now that you have passed through the Warke. It has been increased a thousand fold."

Yes, thought Gando. *But it still might not be strong enough to destroy Rashark.*

"But I... I don't have any magic," exclaimed Eoin. "I can do tricks. Arthur taught me how to, by concentrating my mind. But it was nothing like this." He stared at his forefinger as the magic swirled around the end of it.

This Arthur sounds intriguing, thought Trigon as another blast shot from Eoin and thwacked into a tree twenty meters away, splitting it in half. Gando ducked just in time.

"Human Kind," growled Gando, grabbing Eoin roughly by his arm. "You'd better learn to control your magic or you'll wipe us all out."

Trigon smiled. "He will learn, Gando. As he battles with the Weers and the other beasts that live in the Outlands, he will learn. Come. Let us go to Lela. She will be anxious to meet with the Human Kind."

Shortly Eoin was allowing himself to be led through the trees towards the garden of Aroon. He was growing quickly excited. He looked at his forefinger once or twice, careful to close his hand quickly when he saw the magic swirl around the base of his forefinger, ready to erupt. He still couldn't believe what had happened. He was dying to try it out again, and he was quickly becoming less afraid of the little men. He had noticed some of the elves had looked afraid when the power had blasted from his finger. *At least*, he thought *I'll be able to protect myself*.

⤝❧⤞

At the same time Arthur was emerging from the Warke. As he did, he looked around the dark place he had landed in. The smell was overpowering, and black fanged monsters roamed everywhere, feeding on each other and roaring loudly. *I'm in the wrong place*, he thought. *No one could live here.*

From out of nowhere a beast tore at him, but Arthur was quicker. As he unleashed a blast of magic at it, the bright light tore the beast in two and lit up the whole area. Attracted by the light, smaller beasts near him, with blood oozing from their yawning mouths, turned. Snarling, they began to crawl speedily towards the old man. But Arthur, aware that the Warke was disappearing, did a quick backward flip and dropped into it. Immediately he was sucked away.

I hope I get to the right place this time, he thought as he was propelled through the swirling magical tunnel.

❧

Eoin and his captors reached the garden ten minutes later, and by then Trigon had explained a little of why Eoin had been brought to Eglin. Still unable to take it all in, Eoin stared at the beautiful unicorns that now came galloping down to meet them with Lela leading them.

As she approached, Eoin frowned as he heard silvery voices talking inside his head. One voice was asking, "Mother, who is that creature with the strange ears?"

"Quiet!"

"But mother, look at his ears. They are not like the elves. They—"

"Be quiet, I say! He is a Human Kind, the one who is going to bring your brother, Chalice, home safely."

"Has he great magic, mother?"

"I hope so." *He will need to have it*, she thought to herself. "Now all of you go down to the fruit trees and feed. I must speak with the Human Kind. Go!"

Suddenly the young unicorns galloped straight at Eoin. Just when he thought they were going to trample him into the ground, they veered past him and galloped on down the path to the trees.

Seconds later Eoin was looking up into Lela's face. *I've never seen a horse so beautiful*, he thought, *at least not one with a horn. But it isn't a horse. It's a unicorn. A unicorn*, he thought, *a real unicorn.*

Lela snickered softly. "Welcome, Eoin," she said. "Welcome to the garden of Aroon." The beautiful unicorn studied the little boy. *He is very innocent. I wonder if he will be up for the danger that lies ahead of him?* Her sharp eyes caught the light that glinted from the medal hanging around Eoin's neck. Then she said, "Your name is Eoin isn't it?"

"Ye... yes," stammered Eoin, glancing at the elves.

"Did the Wiself Trigon explain to you why you were brought here?"

"Yes, but..."

Lela looked at Trigon. "He has the magic?" she asked.

"Yes, Lela. Powerful magic, indeed," answered the old elf.

"Powerful enough to destroy Rashark?"

"Rashark?" said Eoin turning to Trigon. "Who the heck is Rashark? You never told me about anyone called, Rashark."

At this Lela neighed loudly and rose on her hind legs. It was obvious she was angry. She glared at Trigon.

"I did not want to frighten the Human Kind," Trigon said quietly looking at Eoin. "He is just a boy, after all."

Lela whinnied softly. "Yes, he is," she said. "But it is better for the young Human Kind to know everything." To Eoin she said, "I will tell you who Rashark is. Rashark is a warlock Weer beast—the most foul, evil monster in our land. His greed for magic has driven him mad. Rashark is merciless to any unicorn his Weers capture and bring to him. Rashark breaks off each of their horns and sucks their magic from it, and thus his power grows. Every day Rashark grows more powerful. If he were to find out that my son Chalice is among the unicorns his Weers have captured recently, the monster would break off my son's golden horn and take his magic. With the power of my son's magic he would be invincible. For you see, my son is the supreme unicorn, and if his magic is taken, then all unicorns will lose their magic. We would all die." She paused and looked at Trigon.

"If the unicorns die, then we elves would perish, too," he said. "You see it is the unicorn's magic that sustains our land. Without it, the monsters that dwell in the Outlands would be able to roam freely. The Weers could come out during daylight and invade our wonderful land, and eventually Rashark would rule it. We would all be better off dead than to be ruled by the evil one."

Lela and the elves studied Eoin as he tried to understand all he had heard.

"Your son, er, Chalice," he said after a few seconds. "Where is he being held captive?"

For the first time, Gando noticed the dull glow of magic coming from Eoin's eyes.

"Away to the north, deep in the Outlands, in Rashark's domain," answered Lela.

"Where the beasts are?" gasped Eoin.

"Yes," answered Lela.

Eoin looked at Lela again. "I don't know where the Outlands are," he said as his newly-strengthened magic worked on his brain, enlightening him to the elves and the unicorn's plight. "I mean—is it very far? I should really be back at the orphanage before it gets dark."

But now his magic brought more enlightenment to him. Horrified, he gasped, "I could be killed, couldn't I?" He looked at the elves anxiously; their eyes confirmed his question. "I... I could be killed." Eoin gulped

Gando thought to himself, *And most probably will be.*

Eoin gulped again. *Killed*, he thought.

❦

Arthur was being tugged and buffeted as he tried using what magic he had left to keep from passing out—and also, to get to where Eoin was. Suddenly he was shot from the Warke and found himself in a desert. Sand stretched as far as he could see in this land below twin bright suns. There was no sign of life. *The wrong place again*, he thought. *I must find Eoin. I must help him.* With another backward flip he was pulled back into the roaring Warke.

❦

The General studied Eoin trying to understand how he must be feeling. *Why should he risk his life?* he thought. *We mean nothing to the Human Kind.* "I will be going with you Human Kind," he said. "My best officer, Drollo, and little Moro—my most experienced tracker—will accompany us as well."

Eoin glared at him. With an angry snort he shouted, "I didn't say I would do it, did I?" He swung to glare at Trigon. "What if I wanted to go back home right now? Would you take me?"

Trigon looked at Lela, and then back at Eoin. "Yes, Human Kind, you would be returned to your land," he said quietly. "We cannot force you to help us. If you wanted to, you could easily kill us all. Your magic is powerful enough to do that. We could not—and would not—force you to help us." He glanced at Lela again, then sighed heavily before saying to Eoin, "But if you really want to return, then I will take you back."

Lela's eyes glistened at these words. With a soft whinny she said, "Human Kind. If you go back to your land without helping us, my son will certainly die. We do not have the magic to face Rashark. You do. There is no one else who can take your place. The Oracle has spoken."

"The... Oracle? What's an Oracle?" asked Eoin.

Trigon quickly explained.

"And out of all the boys in Ireland, it picked me?" asked Eoin.

"Not picked, Human Kind," said Lela. "Only you had magic. You had magic in your land. That magic has increased since you passed through the Warke."

"But I told them I have no magic," said Eoin looking at the Trigon and Gando. "It was Arthur who taught me some tricks and that's all they were, tricks. I could do them if I concentrated hard enough. But they were just tricks."

Lela neighed. "They weren't tricks, Eoin. You do have powerful magic."

"You spoke of this Arthur before," said Trigon. "Who is he?"

"He's an old man I'm friendly with. He taught me to use my mind to do the things I could do. He told me never to show anyone else."

Lela whinnied quietly and her beautiful eyes were suddenly glistening with tears. "Eoin," she whispered, her voice tremulous. "Will you help save my son? Please?" Suddenly a tear rolled from one eye and down her long face. Whinnying softly, she turned away.

Eoin gulped. He felt sorry for the unicorn. *I can't refuse,* he thought. *I can't. But I could be killed.*

❧

Arthur was looking out at the fourth new land since entering the Warke in Ireland. *I must find Eoin,* he thought frantically as he was sucked into the Warke once again, on his way aimlessly to another new world.

❧

As Eoin thought about it, he knew he had to help Lela. He wanted to help. No one had ever needed his help before. Here in Eglin, he was regarded as a savior—a hero, maybe—and he had this *magic*.

He still couldn't believe it was really magic. He studied Lela again, trying to understand how much she loved her son. He wondered if his mother had loved him as much as Lela loved Chalice. It was then that he made up his mind.

He sighed softly, then said, "If you really think I can help, then I will." His heart was pounding as he thought, *What have I done?*

Trigon smiled and Gando nodded, but the General's face was grave. *At least* he thought to himself, *we'll be doing something. Better than standing around just waiting for Rashark to discover Chalice.*

"Thank you, Eoin," said Lela. "Now you must allow Trigon to disguise you. You must be provided with ears."

"Ears?" exclaimed Trigon. He studied Eoin. "Yes—a disguise..."

Eoin was puzzled. "But I have ears."

"Your ears are not like ours," said Trigon. He explained the reason for this as Eoin frowned. "You see Rashark must not know we have brought you—a Human Kind—to our land. The monster would wonder why. He might realize that Chalice is with the other unicorns. Rashark must not know you are Human Kind until you face him."

"Face him? What do you mean?"

"Trigon means that Rashark must be destroyed," said Gando gruffly. He was impatient to get Eoin into the trees. "Now let us go. We must be down in the trees as soon as possible. But first we will see about your ears."

◈

Arthur frowned as he looked around the new land he had entered from the Warke. Trees as thick as houses and as tall as Cathedral spires grew everywhere. Suddenly, the sound of maniacal laughter echoed around the clearing he had standing in. Just as he was making up his mind to leap back into the Warke, a creature with hypnotic, glowing eyes slipped from behind one of the trees.

The creature was green and scaly and had two tiny horns growing from its pointed head. It had a crafty evil look about it. As Arthur was about to leap into the Warke, an arrow thudded into his shoulder. The shock of the pain had him staggering back just beyond the Warke's entrance. Almost passing out from the pain, he was horrified to see three more of the grinning creatures appear from behind another tree.

With their pointed teeth dripping saliva, they crouched as they slipped quickly towards Arthur. As they did, Arthur could feel himself getting weaker, and he knew that if he passed out now he was finished. Quickly he muttered a few ancient words and with a grunt, he waved his hands in front of his body at the same time taking a deep breath. Immediately a glowing protective barrier covered him completely, and he lay back as the frustrated and shrieking creatures tried to break through it to get to him.

But his barrier was holding, and he hoped it would last long enough for him to regain enough strength to search for the Warke that had disappeared again.

CHAPTER SIX

FALSE EARS &
THE FOREST OF CHAMELEO

EOIN SAT BY THE FIRE ON A TINY BASKET CHAIR, watching an old elf woman who was sitting at a low oak table by the only window in the cottage. She was etching out a pair of ears from fine, skin-colored clay. Her wizened hands moved with such incredible dexterity that Eoin was fascinated. Once or twice, the woman glanced at Eoin's ears, then, using a thin bladed knife with a bone handle, she quickly and carefully scraped the clay into shape. As he watched her, Eoin thought about all that had happened to him. He wished that Arthur was here with him. He felt lonely and afraid, and he was regretting now that he had promised to help Lela and the elves.

In just five minutes, the false ears were ready. As she fitted them onto Eoin's ears, the old woman warned, "Human Kind––stay away from water! If your ears get wet, they will lose their shape and break off."

She stood back and studied him for a moment. "Yes I think they're fine. Move your head a little to the left. Yes. Can you hear me?"

Eoin nodded.

Gently, the elf woman squeezed the false ears tighter onto Eoin's ears, then she pulled some of Eoin's long hair around each ear to hide the fine joint. "Would you like to see?" she asked.

Eoin studied his reflection in the hand mirror the woman held in front of him. He did look strange. It was surprising how much he looked like an elf now. He raised and lowered his eyebrows to move his false ears and almost laughed. The false ears did look real...

Just then Gando entered. He allowed a smile to brighten his stern face when he saw Eoin. But a moment later his face was grim again. "Are you finished?" he growled at the old woman.

"His ears are ready and fitted, impatient scoundrel!" said the woman good-naturedly.

"Good. Let's go," Gando said to Eoin. "Drollo and Moro are waiting."

As Gando, Drollo, and another tiny elf who must be Moro the tracker that Gando had spoken of earlier walked through the village with Eoin, the streets were lined with thousands of cheering elves. Many of them shouted, "Good luck!"

A few minutes later when they were out of sight of the village, Gando pulled a light leather tunic from Drollo's haversack and handed it to Eoin, saying, "Wear this, Human Kind. You will look more like an elf."

"Not with those green eyes, he won't," muttered Moro.

"We'll just have to take our chances," growled Gando, giving Moro a cold look. "Lead on."

Skipping lightly ahead, Moro led the way up a winding track and soon they were heading down into the bottom of the valley where a herd of unicorns grazed. As they passed through the unicorns, a voice shouted from the top of the valley.

"Good luck, Human Kind! Good luck!" It was the uniherd. At this greeting, several unicorns neighed and Eoin heard a babble of voices in his head again. "Good luck, Human Kind. Bring the supreme one safely home."

Shortly Eoin and the elves were heading into Chameleo forest. As they jogged quickly through the trees, Eoin saw many strange animals and birds. Once he saw two creatures that had heads like elephants and the bodies of huge bears. They seemed to be friendly enough, though, because the elves ignored them.

The trees in Chameleo forest were tall and straight. Though they were covered in thick leaves, there was plenty of light. Squirrels of many different colors bounded everywhere, and Eoin saw some that were every color of the rainbow.

They had jogged about two miles when they came to a tree that had broken branches lying at its base. As they passed it, Eoin saw a thin branch shaped like a "Y" and stopping, he broke it off. Then, as they walked on, he quickly made a rough sling-shot using the elastic that Arthur had taken from the tomtit's beak.

They had only gone another half-mile when Moro—who had stayed a good bit ahead—came running back. He was holding his forefinger to his lips, telling them to be quiet. "Up ahead," he whispered. "Near the lake. There is something there."

"*Something?*" whispered Gando, looking into the trees.

"The birds are silent," said Moro. "A sign that somebody or something is there... hiding, waiting."

"An ambush?" asked Drollo."

Moro shrugged his shoulders. "Perhaps. I'm not sure, but something is definitely hiding there."

Gando narrowed his eyes as he looked ahead. Then he said, "Right, Moro. You stay here with the Human Kind. Drollo and I will slip ahead to the lake and investigate. Do *not* follow us." He glared at the little elf. "That is an order." Then, with Drollo at his side, the elf General ran quickly and silently out of sight.

Soon they were within sight of the lake that they could easily see through the trees. Now Gando silently signaled for Drollo to go to the left. With their daggers drawn and keeping each other in sight, they edged forward. As they drew closer to the water, they could see no sign of danger. Yet they knew there was danger nearby, for their ears were quivering—a sure warning.

Looking over at Drollo, Gando raised his shoulders. Raising his eyebrows, Drollo shook his head. He could see nothing either, yet their ears still quivered. But they both knew there was definitely danger nearby.

Suddenly from behind they heard a cry. It was Eoin. Immediately the two elves were racing back to Eoin and Moro. Whatever had been at the lake had circled back and was now attacking Eoin and Moro.

The thing that threatened Eoin and Moro was so terrifying that Eoin stood frozen to the ground with fear. In front of him, the little tracker had his knife drawn and was facing the monster. Moro's slanted eyes were glowing as what little magic he had spluttered from his fingers. He knew he had no chance against the monster, and he was hoping Gando and Drollo would show up soon.

And just then, they did. They appeared behind the monster who did not hear them as it glared and roared, its attention focused on the tiny elf.

The monster was a Rhinbuff—a cross between a buffalo and a rhinoceros, but twice as big. It roared loudly again when it saw Gando and Drollo edge quickly around to stand beside Eoin. Gando glanced at the shocked, pale-faced Eoin. *Useless*, he thought as the monster began to paw at the ground with its massive front feet. All the time it roared, then suddenly it lowered its massive head and got ready to charge.

"Look out!" screamed Drollo. "It's going to attack!"

"Use your magic to distract it!" shouted Gando. "Keep it away from the Human Kind! He is not ready."

As the monster scraped its paws on the ground and got ready to launch itself at the elves, Gando and Drollo raised their right hands. Pointing with their forefingers, they allowed short bursts of flashing magic to hit the enraged monster on the head. Roaring even louder as their magic distracted it, the monster tore huge lumps out of the ground and now it began to move slowly towards the elves, swinging its head from side to side.

"Our magic isn't strong enough!" shouted Moro, who was still allowing his magic to hit the monster.

Gando studied the monster. He knew the Rhinbuffs to be ferocious beasts, but they rarely attacked without reason. But then he noticed a white, frothy substance bubbling at the corner of its mouth, and he knew instantly what had made the monster attack. "It's mad!" he screamed. "It's been bitten by a Weer!"

His words sent shudders running up and down Drollo's back and Moro grew pale, but still they kept hitting the monster with their magic. It was having little effect.

"It's no use, General!" shouted Drollo. "We'll have to run for it!"

All this time that the elves had been battling with the monster, Eoin hadn't moved. His eyes were still wide with horror and had never left the ferocious monster's face.

Suddenly it attacked, diving so quickly at the elves that Moro was taken by surprise. The tip of one of its horns caught the little elf, flinging him to one side. Now as Gando and Drollo tried to summon more magic to distract it, the monster lowered its head and glared at the motionless Eoin.

Moaning, Moro lay dazed on the ground. His moaning made Eoin look at him. Suddenly, just as the monster attacked, Eoin became instantly, magically alert. Pointing at it, he caught the Rhinbuff mid-charge with a blast of magic that was so powerful it lifted the surprised monster right off the ground and sent it crashing back into the trees where it lay dying. One of its thick horns had been broken off by Eoin's powerful blast.

Gando looked at Drollo, who was gaping at Eoin. So too was Moro as he struggled to get to his feet.

"Did... did you see?" exclaimed Drollo, going over to Moro to help him.

"Yes," whispered the little elf, looking in awe at Eoin.

Gando smiled as he thought, *the Human Kind is not entirely useless*. He went over to Eoin.

Trembling, Eoin asked, "What... what was th... that?" He pointed into the trees. By then the Rhinbuff was dead.

"A Rhinbuff," said Gando. "Normally they are friendly beasts, but this one was mad. It had been bitten by a Weer." He slapped Eoin on the back, almost knocking him onto his face. "You did well, Human Kind."

"Did I?" said Eoin stupidly. "Yes I did, didn't I?" He began to smile.

"Of course you did," said Drollo, helping Moro over to them. "You saved us all. Our magic was useless against the Rhinbuff, but yours..." He shook his head. "Yours... I've never seen magic so powerful."

Grinning, Eoin looked at his hand, then over at the trees where the monster lay. *It was easy*, he thought to himself.

"It will have to be powerful enough to destroy Rashark when we enter his lair," said Gando, studying Moro now. "Are you able to go on, Moro?" he asked. The elf was pale.

"Yes I'm fine," said Moro bravely. The pain in his arm was bearable.

"Good. Then let's get on," said Gando. "It's time we were further into the Chameleo. We have quite a way to go yet before we reach the mountains. Be alert. I have a feeling there are more beasts about who have been bitten by the Weers."

Eoin frowned at this. His relief at having destroyed the Rhinbuff was quickly vanishing as he thought about the Weers. "Tell me about these Weers," he asked. "What are they like? Are they big? They have to be, if they can bite a monster as big as the Rhinbuff. "

"You will see the Weers soon enough, Human Kind," said Gando gruffly. "Hopefully, you will be strong enough to destroy them."

Eoin thought about this. *Strong?* He looked at his forefinger. It still glowed. *It was easy to kill the Rhinbuff,* he thought to himself. He smiled now. *All I have to do is point my finger at the Weers. My magic will do the rest.* Feeling a lot more confident, he hurried after the elves.

It took Eoin and the elves about ten minutes to jog around the edge of the lake. Just then Moro, whose arm was getting less painful, raised his good arm and pointed, and they came out of the trees. Here was a track the width of a tennis court and bordered by trees. The rough track ran for about a mile then curved out of sight. "We go that way," he said.

As they walked near the middle of the track, Drollo explained to Eoin about Rashark. "The Weers are so loyal to Rashark they would die for him," he said. "Not because they love the monstrous beast, but because they are terrified of him."

"I... I suppose Rashark's big?" asked Eoin. "I mean—have you ever seen him?"

"No," said Drollo. "But I've heard enough about him to know that I probably don't want to."

"Then why are you going to the Outlands with us?" asked Eoin.

"It is my duty," said Drollo with a shrug. "I would die before I gave up now. Rashark has to be destroyed, but if we can steal Chalice back without encountering the monster, all the better."

Gando growled silently. *Without encountering Rashark?* he said under his breath. *Hah. We'd be so lucky.*

As they walked on they failed to see several pairs of slanted eyes watching them from near the top of a cluster of tall oaks. The things that watched them trembled slightly, shaking some leaves onto the ground as the strange creatures sitting on their backs began to whisper silent commands, getting them ready to attack.

⸙

Meanwhile, in a huge underground cavern many miles away, Chalice and about four hundred other unicorns neighed and whinnied nervously as ten Weers came into the large chamber in which they were packed. Two huge pillars—each as round and as thick as towers and as tall as a three-story house—stood at the entrance to this chamber. Horrifying gargoyles covered each pillar and five glowing crystals jutted from each of the rough walls, dully lighting the chamber.

The roof was about ten meters high and crawled with huge black insects that looked like scorpions. The main roof of the underground cavern where the Weers lived was so dark and so high, it was impossible to see what supported the earth and tall oak trees that grew above it on the surface. The cavern was the size of a football stadium, and in the very middle of the flat, smooth floor was a hole so big a house could easily have fit into it. From this hole belched flames, and the smell of sulphur filled the whole cavern.

Chalice snickered fearfully when he saw the Weers lash out at some unicorns near the edge of the herd. It only took seconds for them to cut about twenty of them out from the rest of the herd, driving them towards the entrance to the chamber. The unfortunate unicorn's cries had the others trembling with fear, yet they pressed towards the ferocious Weers to try and save them. But now four of the Weer beasts sprang at them and cracked their whips to keep the neighing, kicking herd back while the six other Weers drove the twenty unicorns out of the chamber. Seconds later, all the Weers had gone.

Chalice neighed and stamped his feet, for he could feel his magic pumping through him. A tear of frustration tumbled down his beautiful boned face. *There is no escape from this terrible place*, he thought as some of the female unicorns near him began to cry.

❧

Shaking his throbbing head and grunting with pain, Arthur sat up. *I must have passed out*, he thought. It was then that he saw that his protective barrier had almost dissolved. He realized the fury of the creature's attack had forced it right back into the trees. Forgetting his injury, the old man stretched to look past the creatures. *Where is it?* He couldn't see where the Warke had been.

He gulped now when he saw several other creatures slip from the trees to join the four who were attacking his barrier. Screeching like banshees, they tore at it until in a few quick seconds a small hole appeared. Arthur knew he did not have the strength to make another barrier. He had to save what little magic he had left to find the Warke and get away. He studied the biggest of the creatures that now pulled a wicked looking knife from the folds of its leathery green skin. Grinning, it placed an elongated finger on the sharp point of the knife. It was obvious what it was going to do.

❧

Chalice was standing near the edge of the herd beside a family of five unicorns. He listened as he heard the youngest unicorn ask her father, "Where did they take those unicorns, Father?"

Her father neighed and glanced at his mate. "How would I know," he snickered angrily.

Suddenly, the sound of loud crying echoed around the chamber. The unicorns nearest to the pillars began to push back to try and get away from the twenty unicorns who had been taken away earlier. They were a sorry sight. Chalice rose on his hind legs to see what the commotion was. His eyes widened with horror as he caught a glimpse of the nearest of the group. Tears were running down its face and its head was almost bent to the ground. Now other unicorns began to cry when they saw what the horrified Chalice had seen. The horns of the twenty unicorns had been broken off. Their magic was gone. Soon the whole herd of unicorns was crying.

In its lair, Rashark heard them and began to roar with laughter. The monster reached for one of the pile of twenty unicorn horns that lay on a filthy cushion. Holding one up to its mouth, Rashark sucked hard on it.

Rashark was truly a monster. It had the head of a wolf with great glistening yellow fangs that dripped with black saliva. Its hands had nails on them as long as canoe paddles. Rashark wore a long black cloak with holes in it to allow room for its hairy muscled arms. The monster's feet were bare and hairy, with toe nails as long as cricket bats.

Rashark was the size of a Council House and around its neck hung a black unicorn horn on a thick gold chain. Now as it sucked the magic from the horn the monster began to glow all over. When the horn was empty, it tossed it over its shoulder into a dark corner of the lair where it clattered among several thousand that lay there.

Reaching for another horn, Rashark smiled as magic dripped from its wet snout onto its chest. *Eventually*, it thought, *my Weers will capture the supreme unicorn. Then when I drain the magic from its horn I will certainly be the most powerful being in all the lands. I will be able to go into the Warke to other lands and destroy all who oppose me. What a time I will have.*

"Ha, ha, ha, ha, ha, ha, ha..." The monster roared with laughter, its mad eyes glowing in the semi-darkness.

Rashark's laughter echoed around the lair reaching the outer chambers where the unicorns still cried.

Chalice shivered as he thought about the twenty unfortunate unicorns that now stood huddled together at the far end of the chamber, too ashamed to mingle with the rest of the herd. No other unicorn would go near them now. In fact, they couldn't even look at them.

What am I going to do? Thought Chalice to himself. *Soon it will be my turn.*

CHAPTER SEVEN

MON-KEE FORT

THE CREATURES THAT WERE HIDING IN THE OAK trees on the edge of the track watching Gando, Drollo, Moro and Eoin were giant bird monsters that now rose silently into the air. Their wings, though massive, vibrated as fast as those of a hummingbird so that the only sound they made was a low hum. Each monster had a wingspan of over ten meters and a head like an owl, only they were as big as a four-door car. The monsters had hooked talons, and thick leather straps were attached to their legs and around their feathered necks. Their passengers, of which there were two, resembled monkeys. They were covered in thick black hair and each of the creatures had a red head that was completely bald. White rings surrounded their curly tails. Now chattering low commands, they guided their feathered mounts in behind Eoin and the elves.

Gando was the first to become aware of them. With a warning scream he turned as the three nearest monsters flew at them, scattering the frightened boy and the elves. The wing of one of the creatures caught the General square on the chest and he was lifted right off his feet and flung about five meters along the ground.

Drollo, with magic flashing along the handle of his sword, cut at the nearest monster, but only just succeeded in slicing a piece of leather from its leg. Moro, who had not quite turned when the attack had begun, had been hit on his injured arm and now lay in agony on the ground. He could only watch helpless as he saw Eoin look at his finger and point. But nothing happened. The boy's eyes widened with shock. He couldn't summon his magic. At the same time, one of the bald-headed riders clubbed him on the head. As Eoin fell, the bird monster grabbed him with its huge talons and rose quickly into the air.

Magic flashed from the frantic Gando and Drollo, but it was not strong enough to do much harm to the bird monsters. Suddenly one of the riders cupped its hands to its mouth and gave a loud screech. Almost immediately, the monsters rose higher into the sky and flew off.

Below Gando and Drollo could only stare with dismay as Eoin was carried away out of sight.

Meantime, Arthur was waiting until the creatures were about to fall on him before summoning his magic. Suddenly he raised his hand and instantly blue magic flared into it, then erupted from his palm. The shock of the blast threw the creatures back. As they fell, Arthur, grunting and still dizzy, scrambled to his feet and stumbled past them. But one of the creatures, squealing in anger, managed to grab at his ankle. Another blast from Arthur had the creature screeching with pain and now the old man stumbled on, his sharp eyes searching for the position of the Warke.

"Where is it?" he muttered frantically, looking all around. He was struggling to keep from fainting, because he knew if he passed out now he was finished. Behind him, he was aware of the creatures recovering. Shrieking with anger they were quickly on their feet. Sweat bubbled on Arthur's pale brow and his face was as white as snow. *I must find the Warke. I must. Oh, where is it?*

He glanced back. Screaming, the horned creatures were racing to catch up with him.

❧

"What are we going to do now?" grunted Moro, nursing his throbbing, painful shoulder. The fall had made it worse.

Gando looked ahead. "We have to go after the Human Kind," he said quietly.

Drollo gaped at the General. "To the mon-kee fort?" he exclaimed. "You *know* that's where they've taken the Human Kind."

Gando nodded.

"Gando, you know the mon-kees hate us. They'd *never* let us get him back now. What are we going to do? Once the Human Kind is inside the mon-kee fort, we've no chance of rescuing him," exclaimed Drollo.

Gando, still looking in the direction the bird monster had taken Eoin, said quietly, "We have to go after him, Drollo. We must try and explain to them why the Human Kind is here." He turned to see the look on Drollo's face. "What else can we do?" he said. Then turning to Moro he said, "I'm ordering you to return, Moro."

The little elf frowned. "But—"

"Your shoulder needs attention. Besides, you will slow us up. We have to move fast now. Drollo and I must reach the fort as quickly as we can. It is near dark. The Weers will be roaming soon. It will be dangerous."

Moro grunted painfully as he shifted his arm into a more comfortable position.

"When you return," said Gando, "tell Trigon and the others what has happened. Tell them to send a hundred of my best soldiers after us. We will meet them outside the mon-kee fort." Gando gently touched Moro's good arm. "Go now, brave Moro." Then swinging to look at Drollo he said, "Let us get on."

Moro watched as the General and Drollo began to race quickly along the track, and then with a sigh he turned and began the long trot home.

⸎

Arthur swung to face the creatures bearing down on him. Two of them had already fitted arrows to their bows, but in an instant Arthur had unleashed more magic at them. The bows shattered and the deadly arrows fell to the ground. Arthur now blasted at the other creatures, and as he did so, he knew that the power of his magic was getting weaker. He had stopped them for a moment, but quickly they began to separate as they got ready to attack again.

Two more blasts hit the nearest creatures, but Arthur was dismayed when this time they seemed to recover more quickly. He blasted at them again. As he did, he took another quick look around, searching for the exact place the Warke had been. He almost fell over it. The faint outline of the Warke was shimmering beside a low bush. Unleashing two more blasts at the ground in front of the attacking creatures, Arthur turned and stumbled towards the Warke, waving his hands in front of it and mumbling the ancient magical words.

As the Warke opened and began to pull at him, Arthur turned back towards the creatures. He did not want any of them coming into the Warke after him. Raising both of his hands with an effort that made him cry out, he blasted as much magic as he could summon at the creatures. As they were flung back, the old man swung around and leapt into the Warke. But as he was whisked to safety, he passed out.

⚬❧⚬

Mon-kee fort was constructed of hundreds of tiny huts all made from saplings, with the bark stripped from them. The huts were built in a huge circle around the tall wooden statue of a giant mon-kee. On the outside of the ring of huts were the actual fortifications—thick-trunked trees that rose over a hundred meters into the sky. A massive gate at one end of the fort was made of thinner tree trunks. A wide platform was constructed around the perimeter of the fort, and long ladders made of rope dangled from the platform on which over five thousand mon-kees stood guard. These guards had bald, blue heads and carried long spears. They all watched as the hunting party returned, landing near the statue. Quickly hundreds of mon-kees began to crowd around the hunting party, curious to see Eoin, who now lay on the ground, but was quickly recovering. A few seconds later, after a couple of hard prods from some of the mon-kees near him, Eoin groaned and opened his eyes.

Rising unsteadily to his feet, Eoin looked around. Feeling the lump on the back of his throbbing head, he gaped at the strange, excited creatures that thronged around him, jabbering loudly and pointing at him. The words, "He's only an elf," came to Eoin. "What good will he be? Why does Orca want him?"

Suddenly the sounds of their words died away as the mon-kees in front of Eoin parted to allow the strangest creature he had seen since he arrived in Eglin to get through. The creature was bulky and resembled a gorilla. It was bald with a pink wrinkled head. Its powerful body was covered in long, white silky hair. It wore small glasses that sat on its broad nose beneath two fierce red eyes.

Eoin gaped at the creature as it studied him. Then he heard a mon-kee behind the white-haired one shriek, "He's an elf! We've only captured an elf. We've captured the wrong one." The mon-kee who had shrieked was thinner but bigger than the other mon-kees and wore a red cloak.

"No," growled the white haired creature. "He's not an elf."

The thinner creature with the red cloak stretched its neck forward to peer closely at Eoin. "Not an elf? Orca, you have made a mistake. You are wrong."

At this statement, the mon-kees who were gathered around them gasped.

Orca, the white haired mon-kee, turned to the thin mon-kee. "A mistake, Tark?" he growled. He swung back to Eoin and smiled. Eoin gulped when he saw Orca's long yellow fangs.

"I am not wrong. He is a Human Kind," Orca said quietly and pointed at Eoin. "Human Kind."

The words, "Human Kind," were echoed by all the mon-kees—except the one with the red cloak. Then Orca said, "Human Kind, come closer."

"Wha... what do you want?" asked Eoin, moving a step back from Orca.

"I certainly do not want to harm you, if that's what you're thinking," said Orca his eyes burning into Eoin's. "You know that."

Eoin frowned as he studied Orca. *Yes* he thought. *I don't believe he wants to hurt me, but...*

"Do as we say, elf," snapped the thin mon-kee, coming closer.

Suddenly Orca turned and gave an enormous roar that startled Eoin and made the other mon-kees cower back a little. "Tark!" he roared to the thin mon-kee, "if you do not keep quiet I will lose my temper! I told you, he is *not* an elf. He is a Human Kind."

Tark glared at Orca, but buried his thin head into his narrow shoulders and backed down. Then he turned to glare at several mon-kees nearby who had giggled at him.

"Come closer, Human Kind," said Orca again.

Hesitantly Eoin took a step towards Orca. Suddenly, before he could dodge away, Orca tore at him with his massive hands.

CHAPTER EIGHT

THE CURSELM

THE ELF SOLDIERS GUARDING THE ENTRANCE TO the Warke swung around when they heard a groan come from inside the cave. Grabbing for their weapons, they crowded around the entrance. Someone— or something—had come through the Warke and was inside. Their leader was just about to command twenty of his best soldiers to rush inside when Arthur staggered from the cave and collapsed at their feet.

"Ge... get Trigon," gasped the leader of the guards as everyone gaped at Arthur. The old man appeared dead.

The shock as Orca crumpled his clay ears to bits startled Eoin.

"Human Kind!" cried several mon-kees moving back a little from Eoin.

"Yes!" shouted Orca. "Human Kind! Now he can use his great magic to destroy the Curselm!"

"Cu... Curselm?" stuttered Eoin as the mon-kees cheered. Suddenly, before he could stop it, his left hand opened and blast after blast of magic roared into the sky. The terrified mon-kees backed further away from him.

Eoin held his hand open for several seconds when he realized he was frightening the bald-headed creatures. Suddenly, he swung and pointed at a trough of water. A blast burst from his finger, shattering it to pieces. The water splashed around the nearest mon-kees to it.

But smiling and unafraid, Orca stayed where he was. "Your magic is powerful, Human Kind," he said as Eoin closed his hand.

Feeling less afraid now, Eoin snapped, "If you try to hurt me I'll blast you all to smithereens." Though he had threatened them, Eoin didn't think he could hurt any of the mon-kees, unless they attacked him.

"We do not wish to harm you, Human Kind," said Orca quietly. "I have told you this. Please, Human Kind, forgive us for the way you have been brought here. But you see, we had an urgent reason for seeking your help."

Eoin narrowed his eyes as the thought came to him. "You knew I wasn't from Eglin?"

"Yes, I knew," said Orca.

"Then you must know why I was brought here?"

"No," said Orca. "That I do not know. I thought you had been brought to help the elves destroy the Weers and Rashark. What other reason would you have been brought through the Warke?"

"I was brought to save Chalice?" said Eoin quietly.

"Chalice, the supreme unicorn? But he is safe in the garden of Aroon with his mother the great Lela, is he not?" exclaimed Orca.

"No. Chalice has been captured along with other unicorns by the Weers. Rashark does not know yet that

Chalice is with them. You see, the Wiselfs had Chalice dyed so that he looked like the other unicorns," explained Eoin. "The Wiselfs had him put with the main herd so that his magic might grow more quickly. That is why I was disguised like an elf. If Rashark knew I had been brought here to save Chalice, then it would search the unicorns it has captured and it would soon find Chalice and kill him. Then it would take Chalice's magic. Rashark would become so powerful no one could destroy it."

Tark listened with the others a scowl on his face. He was thinking about revenge. Orca and the Human Kind had made him look foolish. As Eoin explained why he had been brought to Eglin, an idea came to Tark about how he could have revenge and also become the leader of his tribe.

Orca rubbed his chin. "We must talk about this some more," he said, holding out his hand. "Come, Human Kind."

Eoin pulled back. "Where?" he asked.

"To the Council Hut. This must be discussed with the others. Perhaps we can help you."

As Eoin followed Orca, Tark, and several other big mon-kees, he wondered why his magic hadn't worked when they had attacked. He remembered thinking his magic would come, but something had prevented it. He wondered where Gando and the other elves were, and wished they were with him.

Trigon was gaping at Arthur. Bending, he gently pulled the cap from Arthur's head. Arthur's long, white hair fell around his face, exposing his pointed left ear.

The soldiers gasped and looked at each other when they saw that Arthur was an elf.

"It's Dardo!" exclaimed one of the other Wiselfs when he recognized him.

"Quickly," said Trigon. "Carry him to the healing place."

In a few seconds several soldiers were carrying Dardo along a smooth track to a sheltered grove of chestnut trees that grew nearby. Trigon and the other Wiselfs were delighted that Dardo had returned, but they could see he was very seriously ill. They watched now as the Healer— an old elf with a long beard and red eyes—took a glowing stone shaped like an acorn from a huge stone jar. He muttered ancient healing words and passed the glowing stone back and forth over Dardo's still body.

After a few minutes of examining Dardo, the Healer said to the others, "He has been poisoned by the arrow. It must be removed at once. When it is, I will use the cleansing magic of the acornia. It should draw out the poison."

To Trigon he said, "He is very near the long sleep. It will take much inner healing on his part to save him."

⚜

Gando and Drollo were making their way down through the trees to the fort. Gando reckoned they had about three miles to go, but he had no plan to help Eoin and he was wondering what he was going to do when he got there. *Perhaps*, he thought bravely, *they will exchange my life for his. The mon-kees have always wanted my death.*

⁓⁂⁓

The Wiselfs held their breaths as the Healer stood above Dardo, his legs spread apart to brace himself. Then, with blue magic pulsating from his right hand, he gripped the feathered end of the arrow. Placing his other hand on Dardo's chest, he took a deep breath and with one swift movement, he jerked the arrow free. As everyone studied Dardo, the old elf gave a deep sigh, but his eyes remained closed.

Trigon bent closer and studied him. *I wonder where he's been?* he thought. *What strange things has he seen?* He stepped back to watch as the Healer placed the glowing acornia right in the center of Dardo's wound. As the Healer placed both his hands, with his fingers spread apart around the acornia, blue magic spluttered from them. Dardo's body vibrated violently for a few seconds and as he did the acornia gave off a sucking sound. Suddenly, Dardo's face turned completely white.

With a worried frown Trigon looked at the Healer.

"I've done all I can," said the Healer, removing the acornia that had stopped glowing. "It's now up to Dardo's inner force. The poison is drawn from his wound. All we can do now is wait."

Trigon and the others studied the pale-faced, oldest elf in the land. They had seen the long sleep before and not one of the Wiselfs thought Dardo would recover.

On thick mats on the floor Eoin, Orca, Tark and about twenty other mon-kees sat in a circle in the Council Hut.

"I thought the reason we captured the Human Kind was to get him to destroy the Curselm," screamed Tark.

"Yes!" shouted another mon-kee.

Several others nodded.

Orca looked around them. "That was the reason we captured him. But now we must forego that reason. We must help the Human Kind save the supreme unicorn."

"You don't *really* believe that old tale that when the supreme unicorn dies, *all* the unicorns will die, do you?" sneered Tark. "It's rubbish! The elves have spread this lie to further their own ends. We captured this Human Kind to destroy our most feared enemy, the Curselm, and I say *that* is what he has to do."

Tark looked around the circle. He was delighted to see nearly all the mon-kees there were nodding in agreement. *Perhaps now would be a good time to challenge Orca for leadership of my tribe*, he thought, turning triumphantly to the white mon-kee.

Suddenly Orca rose to his feet. "Ahhhhhh!" he roared. "Don't you fools understand? Destroying the Curselm would mean *nothing* if the supreme unicorn is killed! It is the unicorns who keep the magic in our land. If Chalice dies, all unicorns will die. *We* will all die."

He glared at Tark. "It is not an old tale, Tark. It is written in the annals of history. The magic will die if the unicorns die!" Looking around the others he added, "Rashark would then destroy us all. We have to help the Human Kind save the supreme unicorn. We—"

Suddenly, there was a commotion outside. Bursting into the Council Hut came several highly agitated mon-kees.

"The Curselm!" one of them shouted. "It's broken through the gate! It's already inside our fort! We're doomed!"

Eoin gaped as all the mon-kees, followed by Orca, raced from the hut. Quickly he followed them outside.

Outside he almost choked with horror when he saw the monster that was the Curselm towering above. The huge mon-kee fort gate was in splinters and several mon-kees lay dead around it. Other mon-kees were running around the fort in panic. Eoin gave a start when he felt a hand on his shoulder. It was Orca.

"Human Kind," he said. "It's up to you now. You will have to destroy the Curselm first, after all."

Eoin gulped. "Destroy..." He gaped up at the monstrous thing that was the Curselm, then looked at his finger. There was no sign of his magic. It wouldn't come. It wouldn't come.

CHAPTER NINE

UNITED

WHEN GANDO AND DROLLO WERE ABOUT HALF a mile from the mon-kee fort, Gando suddenly stopped. Holding a hand to one of his ears, he whispered, "Listen!"

The loud roar of the Curselm came to them.

"Come on!" screamed Gando, suddenly breaking into a run. "Whatever it is, the Human Kind might need our help."

❦

The Healer lay dozing in the corner of the peaceful grove. Only Trigon was awake. Five of the Wiselfs had gone to get some sleep, and two others were dozing beside him. Trigon examined Dardo. He was as pale as ever. Dardo was so still that Trigon could not see if he was breathing. He sighed now as he thought about the old elf, the wisest of them all. Dardo had always seemed to know ahead of time what was going to happen. Though all the Wiselfs had seven senses, Dardo seemed to possess more, and it was only through his amazing visionary sense that they were able to keep moving the main herd of unicorns to different parts of the land to keep them safe from the Weers.

But when Dardo disappeared into the Warke, the Weers were able to surprise them. In the two years since Dardo's disappearance, the evil beasts had stolen over three thousand unicorns from the smaller herds. By bringing the main herd to the valley outside Derrylyn village, the Wiselfs believed they would be safe there. *How wrong we were*, thought Trigon, sighing. He was still thinking about it when one of the Wiselfs came running into the grove.

"Trigon, Moro has returned."

"Returned?" exclaimed Trigon jumping to his feet. "Is everything——?"

"He's outside the grove. He says the mon-kees have captured the Human Kind. Gando and Drollo have gone after him to Mon-kee fort. Gando has given orders that a hundred of his best soldiers are to meet him at the fort."

Trigon frowned. "Mon-kee fort," he whispered as he hurried out to question Moro.

❧

The monster the mon-kees called the Curselm was indeed an elm; a giant living elm tree over seventy meters tall with black magic rippling all over its branches and trunk. It moved slowly on its thick, twisted, snake-like roots.

Eoin gulped as he stared up at the Curselm's evil face. The thick trunk of the elm had huge black knotholes for eyes that glared all around at the fleeing mon-kees. The Curselm had a bigger knothole for its mouth that was as wide as a bus, and from which came its ear piercing roars. Inside its mouth, Eoin could see the Curselm's teeth—jagged branches, with thorns as big and as sharp as knives. Its long branches, like a thousand shuddering arms, reached for the screaming and terrified mon-kees.

Eoin shouted a late warning when he saw it grab at several mon-kees who were not quick enough to dodge away from its snapping branches. Whipping around their bodies, the Curselm crushed them and then flung them right out of the fort. Now as the mon-kees ran screaming from the fort through secret hatchways built into the walls, the Curselm's knothole eyes turned to glare at Eoin, who stood beside the Council Hut.

Just behind Eoin stood Orca. They where on their own. Tark had also fled.

By then Gando and Drollo had reached the fort. The terrified, fleeing mon-kees ignored them as they rushed past.

"What's frightened them?" asked Drollo.

Gando didn't answer, but quickly made his way to one of the secret exits. As they pushed through it, they almost bumped into several more fleeing mon-kees who were too frightened to do anything but run.

Seconds later, the elves were running inside the fort.

"What is it?" gasped Drollo when they saw the Curselm.

"I've heard of it," said Gando as he stared at the tiny figure of Eoin, who stood almost beneath the monster. "It's the ancient cursed elm, the mon-kees most feared and evil nightmare. It never comes to our part of the land. It needs to feed here. No wonder the mon-kees captured the Human Kind. They needed him to destroy the Curselm."

As they ran towards Eoin, the elves saw the Curselm reach a branch down to grab at him.

"He's too, frightened to move!" shouted Drollo.

"Yes," said Gando. "Your magic! Use you magic!" he shouted at Eoin.

His shouting distracted Eoin. As he concentrated, reaching deep down into his body to call his magic, he thought, *I have to help. I'm needed.*

As the Curselm's branch twisted around Eoin's body, magic suddenly hummed around his arm and then flickered from his fingers. He easily snapped the branch away.

Roaring with anger and pain, the Curselm whipped again at Eoin. But now powerful magic was ripping from Eoin towards the giant monster tree. The flash and power of his magic was so bright that Orca and the elves had to shade their eyes.

Zap! Zap! Zap! Zap! Four blasts shot at the nearest of the Curselm's branches, severing them. They fell around Eoin.

Orca and the two elves moved back now and watched as more magic blasted out from all over Eoin's body in one great shaft. It thwacked into the Curselm's face and the giant monster tree shuddered until its shuddering became a violent trembling. More magic erupted from Eoin, not only hitting the Curselm's trunk, but also the monster's roots. As it did, the Curselm's roaring grew louder—but this time it was with pain. Now it tried to move back, but its roots were almost destroyed and it could only stand where it was and thrash with its branches as Eoin kept up his magical barrage.

"Look!" shouted Drollo pointing.

Orca, only now aware of the elves, watched with them as the monster began to slowly sink into the ground; deeper and deeper until more than half its trunk and all of its mouth was covered. Abruptly Eoin's magical barrage stopped. As it did, the Curselm became silent and still. Everyone studied it. What remained of the Curselm's face seemed to be smiling.

Silently Orca pointed. A tiny blue bird had flown from outside the fort and had just landed on one of the Curselm's branches. The tree shook slightly and its face seemed to smile even more, then two more birds flew onto another branch. In seconds, hundreds of birds were flitting happily around the tree.

"The curse has been lifted from it," said Orca, walking from the elves over to Eoin.

"Look," said Eoin, pointing at the tear-like substance that oozed from one of the elm's eyes and ran down its trunk to soak into the ground. It had found its resting place here in the mon-kee fort.

"It will harm us no more," said Orca quietly.

As he spoke the other mon-kees began to return, and it was only when Drollo turned to speak to Gando that the elves realized they were surrounded.

꩜

At the same time a hundred soldiers were heading for Mon-kee fort. Trigon had watched them disappear into the trees. *The Weers will be roaming soon*, he thought. It was getting dark. He shuddered as he headed back to the grove to see how Dardo was.

When he arrived, he saw that the Healer was still asleep. Slipping to the back of the grove where Dardo lay, he was shocked to find there was no sign of him. Dardo was gone.

CHAPTER TEN

BETRAYED

Pointing at Gando and Drollo, Tark—who had also returned—screamed, "Kill the elves!"

Other mon-kees quickly gathered around.

Suddenly with a loud roar, Orca leapt at Tark and in an instant he had cuffed the thin mon-kee to the ground. "Do not harm the elves!" he shouted. "They are friends of the Human Kind!"

He pointed to the elm. "See!" he shouted. "See what the Human Kind's great magic has done! See our most feared enemy, the Curselm, is no more. It is a harmless tree. The great power of the Human Kind has lifted the elm's curse. He has saved us."

Everyone studied the tree. It was covered in singing birds of every color, and already some young mon-kees were clambering up into its branches.

"Hooray! Hooray! Hooray!" cheered the mon-kees, and then they began to shout and dance with joy.

Eoin looked at the beautiful elm tree, then at his fingers that still glowed with magic, and smiled. He was beginning to feel a lot easier now about his adventures. His magic had come just when he needed it.

As they watched the mon-kees dance, Gando looked up at the sky. "It is getting dark," he said quietly. Then turning to Eoin he said, "We must move on towards the Outlands—quickly. We have a way to go yet."

Eoin's smile faded as he realized that the day was almost over, and by now they would be missing him at the orphanage. *They'll think I've run away*, he thought. He felt for his medal and gently rubbed it.

"Why don't you wait until morning?" said Orca. "Our Owlers will fly you to wherever you want to go." He glared at Tark, who had risen to his feet. The red-cloaked mon-kee glared back at him, but said nothing.

"No," said Gando. "We do not want Rashark to see us. We must be stealthy. We might be spotted during daylight. We must go now. We must get well into the trees. The path to the mountains is a good distance beyond them."

As they said a quick goodbye, they saw that some of the mon-kees had already begun work on building a new gate.

"Come," said Gando, gently pushing Eoin towards the exit. Still thinking about the orphanage, Eoin walked across the fort, with Drollo following.

"Watch out for the Weers!" warned Orca. "And other beasts," he added quietly as he watched them head into the trees. Then turning to the mon-kees repairing the gate, he roared, "Hurry! We must repair the gate. It's nearly dark. The Weers will be roaming."

The mention of the beasts was enough to make the mon-kees work faster.

While Orca was distracted, Tark was busy untying the leather thong that kept one of the Owlers tied to its perch. "I'll show Orca," he snarled to himself, pulling sharply on the leash. A few seconds later he was sitting on top of the Owler and rising above the fort, flying towards the Outlands.

"Rashark will reward me well for my information," he muttered smugly. "When I tell him about the Human Kind and the supreme unicorn, he will reward me very well."

Tugging hard on the reins, he guided his Owler up into the mountains. As he flew he thought about how he had used his Owler to seek out the herds of unicorns for Rashark's Weers. Once he had even gone to Rashark's lair to tell him about the big herd in Raggadan valley, and he had been well rewarded. Of course, there were other mon-kees who did the same, and they, too, had been well rewarded. Some of them had disappeared with the Weer gold to live in another part of the land, but Tark had stayed. The only reward Tark really desired was to be the leader of his tribe. That was the main reason he even helped the Weers. He would do anything—risk anything—even his life, to become leader of his tribe.

⸙

Meanwhile, led by Gando, Eoin and Drollo were jogging quickly through the trees. Ten minutes later it was dark, and Gando had slowed them to a fast walk. Even so, Eoin was growing tired. It was a good twenty minutes later before Gando noticed that Eoin was lagging behind.

"Human Kind," he snapped, stopping. "We have to get on. There is not much time left."

"Yes, I know," said Eoin. "I'm sorry, Gando. It's just that I'm very tired. If we could rest for a little while, I'll be able to keep up with you."

Gando scowled, but a glance at Drollo's raised eyebrows silently told him that Eoin needed to rest. "Very well," he said. "We'll rest for a few minutes, then we must get on."

As Gando and Drollo sat beside each other with their backs against a tree, Eoin lay down on the soft, mossy ground. Almost at once he was asleep. Nodding towards him, Drollo said, "The Human Kind is sleeping."

Gando rose to waken Eoin, but suddenly changed his mind and sat down again. "We'll let him sleep for a while. We'll need him to be alert when we get to the Outlands."

Drollo shivered as he thought about Rashark's domain. "Gando," he whispered, "we don't have much hope of saving Chalice, do we? I mean, even with the Human Kind's powerful magic, we could still be too late."

Gando sighed. "There is still hope, Drollo," he said. "And besides, anything is better than just waiting until Chalice is killed, isn't it?"

Drollo sighed, too. "Yes," he agreed quietly.

"I mean," said Gando. "I'd rather die trying to save Chalice than just wait in Derrylyn village for Rashark to come and destroy us." He smiled grimly. "I hate waiting. I've always been impatient."

Drollo smiled at him. "Perhaps impatience is what makes you the great General you are."

Gando smiled back at him. "Perhaps." Suddenly he stiffened. "Drollo," he whispered as he scanned the darkness around them. Both elves could feel their ears quivering. "We are being watched." Slowly he rose to his feet.

Drollo, looking around, rose beside him, then each elf slowly withdrew their swords, their magic already flickering into the handles.

Suddenly a monstrous, dark figure stumbled from behind a tree, and as it did both elves moved apart. Then behind another tree more dark figures appeared.

"Weers," gasped Drollo.

⁂

Tark's heart began to pound with fear as he guided the Owler down into the valley between the mountains. In thirty seconds he was dismounting and hurrying into the cavern. The dark shapes of Weers watched him and some moved, growling along with him as he hurried to his destination.

Tark, though still terrified of the Weers, knew they would not dare harm him in case they would incur their master's wrath. Making his way past the chamber where the unicorns were herded, he heard the anguished moaning of the poor creatures that had already lost their horns. He shivered as a new thought came to him. What if Rashark had already discovered the supreme unicorn and had taken its magic? Rashark would have no more need of him, and his information would be useless to the monster he feared more than he had the Curselm.

He slowed now, suddenly reluctant to get to Rashark's lair. But a minute later the dark shapes moved away as he reached it. Outside, the mon-kee hesitated. He was about to take a deep breath and enter the lair when Rashark's booming voice said, "Come in, little thing. You must have very important information for me to come to my lair again."

Tark gulped and trembling with fear, he stumbled through the massive open door.

Rashark lay on a carpet of unicorn hides. All around the monster lay horns from the unicorns it had drained earlier. As Tark drew nearer, Rashark widened its eyes to show the mon-kee how much magic it had consumed. Tark gaped up at Rashark when he saw how much power glowed from the monster's eyes. *Has the monster found Chalice already?* he thought, horrified.

"Yes," said Rashark smiling. "You see it, don't you? My magic *is* powerful. But it is nothing compared to how strong I will be when I consume the supreme unicorn's magic. Soon I will have it. Then, ha, ha, ha, ha, ha... I will go out into the land and destroy every living thing in it. Ha, ha, ha, ha, ha, ha, ha..." Rashark's laughter grew louder when it saw the fear in Tark's face.

The mon-kee trembled as the monster's booming laughter echoed around the lair. As if pleased at their master's joy, several Weers roared loudly.

Now Rashark sat up. Saliva trickled from his yawning mouth and it licked its teeth as it studied the little mon-kee. "Well?" it roared. "Have you found out where the elves are hiding the supreme unicorn?"

Tark gulped. His mouth was dry, but he managed a smile. "I bring information that will please you, great Rashark," he said.

The monster narrowed its eyes, trying hard to suppress its irritation at the bald-headed creature as Tark said, "What would be the thing you desire most, great one?"

Suddenly a beam of magic shot from one of Rashark's eyes and caught Tark by the tail. Screaming with pain as the magic burned him, Tark was upended and drawn up towards Rashark's mouth.

"Little thing!" roared Rashark. "I am not interested in riddles. Tell me what brought you here now or I will crunch you like a kernel."

Though terrified, Tark shouted, "Let me go, then I will tell you how you can get the magic you desire most!"

"Conditions!" roared Rashark, opening its mouth to swallow the squirming mon-kee.

"No—don't!" screamed Tark. "It's Chalice!" he cried. "I can tell you where the supreme unicorn is!"

Rashark's eyes glowed brightly. "Tell me!" boomed the monster.

Tark hesitated. He was tempted to demand a reward, but too terrified to make the monster any angrier. However, his greed overcame his fear. "You must reward me. You must promise me that when you have the supreme unicorn's great magic, that you will make me the leader of all my tribe!"

Suddenly Rashark reached out to touch the damp wall beside it. The scraping sound as it drew its terrible sharp claws along the wall echoed throughout the cavern. The sound was so shrill it hurt the mon-kee's ears. "Tell me!" roared Rashark. The monster's voice told Tark that to bargain for the information any longer would mean a terrible death.

"The supreme unicorn you seek is among the captured unicorns. He has been dyed to disguise him!" shouted Tark.

Suddenly Rashark released Tark. With a loud thud he hit the ground. Groaning, he rose to his feet. At the same time so did Rashark.

"Two elves are on their way to rescue Chalice!" Tark shouted angrily.

"Elves!" roared Rashark glaring down at the mon-kee. "They wouldn't dare! How could they hope to get into my domain and out again alive? Their magic is not powerful enough."

"They have brought a Human Kind into Eglin!" shouted Tark. "Through the Warke and his magic is great. He easily overpowered the Curselm. His magic is as powerful as yours!" shouted the mon-kee, pleased that Rashark looked shocked.

"A Human Kind?" snarled Rashark, scraping a long fingernail along its chin. "And you say they are on their way here to rescue the accursed Chalice?"

"Yes," said Tark.

Slowly Rashark began to smile. "Where are they now?" he asked.

"In the trees beyond the mountains," answered Tark.

"The trees. Well my Weers will soon find them. They will soon smell them out. They won't last long," said Rashark.

"Your Weers will be useless against the Human Kind's magic!" said Tark. "I have seen the power of it."

"Useless?" Suddenly Rashark pointed at Tark and screaming with pain, the mon-kee was lifted into the air. "So you think *my* magic would be *useless* against the Human Kind, do you?" roared Rashark as Tark rose right up until he was level with the monster's glaring eyes.

"No!" screamed Tark glancing down. A fall from this height would surely kill him.

Rashark noticed the fear on his face as Tark looked down. The monster smiled. "Little thing, are you afraid to fall?"

"Ye... yes," gasped Tark.

"Good, good," said Rashark, licking its lips. "Then I will not let you fall." Suddenly the monster flicked its finger and Tark shot screaming upwards into the roof of the lair. The speed with which he hit the wooden struts that supported the ceiling killed him instantly. His limp body stuck to the wood for a few seconds, then fell with a splatter at Rashark's feet.

"Ha, ha, ha, ha, ha, ha," laughed Rashark. "Ha, ha, ha, ha!" Suddenly he stopped laughing as he remembered. *Human Kind*, it thought. *Human Kind*, and for a second or two the monster grew afraid, but roaring for its Weer attendants it headed for the chamber to find Chalice.

CHAPTER ELEVEN

WEERS

EOIN WAS STILL SLEEPING SOUNDLY AS GANDO and Drollo backed towards him.

"Human Kind!" screamed Gando as the five growling beasts, crouching low, moved to attack.

Each Weer was over two and a half meters tall. Their wolf-like heads were streaked with white and black hair, and they had enormous, curved canine teeth that dripped with red saliva. Their blood-red eyes were slanted and the terrifying, crafty look on their faces made them look even more fearsome. They were obviously cunning. Howling, they moved closer, their muscled hairy arms ripping and tearing at the air in front of them.

Suddenly, as a moon appeared from behind a cloud, they stopped their advance. Looking up at the moon, they howled loudly. As Gando and Drollo glanced at each other, the Weers' terrifying howls woke Eoin. Rubbing his eyes, he sat up. Immediately he became terrified when he saw the five beasts that again crouched to attack.

"Human Kind!" screamed Gando as he slashed at the arm of the nearest Weer. "Use your magic! Destroy them!"

But Eoin was petrified. He couldn't move and he was too frightened to even concentrate. But when Gando screamed again, he steeled himself and tried to call his magic as the Weers slipped closer. He took another deep breath but it was no use. The magic wouldn't come.

What's wrong? He thought. *Where's my magic? Does it only come when I'm angry?* And he wasn't angry. He was afraid.

Suddenly one of the beasts leapt at Gando, and snarling and grunting, they rolled over and over on the ground. Gando, nimble as ever, just managed to roll onto his feet while cutting at the beast's head with his sword. With a painful howl the Weer crawled away, but two others leapt to take its place. Slashing at them, Gando backed closer towards Eoin.

"Human Kind," he grunted. "You have to help us! We're no match for the beasts. There are too many of them. Use your magic!"

Suddenly there was a scream. It was Drollo. A Weer had suddenly leapt at him and sank its teeth into his shoulder, but as quick as a flash and with blue magic flickering around his sword, Gando leapt to his defense, cutting at the Weer's sinewy neck. With a croaking growl it pulled away from Drollo, who sank to the ground. His face twisted with pain as another Weer leapt to tear the unfortunate elf to pieces. Gando fought to keep the three others back.

"Human Kind!" he screamed. "Help us! Use your magic! Human Kind!"

Rashark was studying the herd of terrified unicorns, saliva tricking down its chest. With around forty Weers gathered behind him, the monster roared. "I have been told that the supreme unicorn Chalice is among you!"

Rashark's eyes narrowed as it watched to see if any of the neighing unicorns would look in Chalice's direction and give him away, but Chalice was standing near the middle of the herd surrounded by ten of the biggest unicorns.

"I want him!" roared Rashark. "I want him to show himself to me now!"

The monster's roaring had the frightened unicorns neighing louder. Some of the braver ones, though, rose on their hind legs to show defiance to the monster. They would not betray Chalice.

Rashark scowled and with a loud bellow, it shot a blast of black magic towards the middle of the herd, killing five of them. Raising his two hands, Rashark prepared to kill more unicorns when suddenly he realized, *I could kill Chalice*. Rashark knew it needed the supreme unicorn alive to take his magic.

Lowering his hands, he roared at the herd. "If you do not give up the supreme Chalice, I will tear you all to pieces myself." Suddenly he grabbed the nearest big unicorn. With another hand Rashark ripped its horn from its head then flung the horrified creature back into the herd. Magic dripped from the end of the horn as Rashark raised it to its mouth, then sucked hard. The feeling of extra power as the unicorn's magic seeped into the monster had it trembling with delight. It held up the horn. "When I take the supreme unicorn's magic, I will be the greatest being in the universe." Rashark narrowed its eyes at the unicorns. "I will have the supreme's horn eventually. The magic will eventually be mine!" he roared as he clenched and unclenched his claws.

Rashark looked around the herd. *They will not give up Chalice*, he thought. The monster was impatient to have the young unicorn's magic now that it knew Chalice was with the herd. It would take the monster a whole day or more to go through the herd one by one, breaking off and sucking all their horns. Then a thought occurred to him and he began to smile. *The Seeker*, he thought, *of course. I will send one of my Weers to get it. It will be back within an hour. The Seeker will uncover Chalice.*

"I will return in one hour," he roared. "And if by then I have not been presented with Chalice, I will come among you and tear you all to pieces until I find him."

Suddenly the monster pointed at the wall behind the unicorns. A blast of the most powerful magic ripped a gaping hole in the rock. The Weers, who stood near the edge of the herd, cheered as their master roared, "One hour!" then walked away. A few seconds later, one of the Weers was heading out of the cavern to a dark place up in the mountains to fetch the Seeker for its master.

Chalice shivered. *An hour*, he thought to himself. His magic rippled up and down his body, unseen. *One hour...*

⚜

Eoin was watching Gando battling with the Weers. At the same time he was trying to concentrate on summoning his magic. *Why won't it come?* Sweat stood out on his pale brow with the effort. What was wrong? Before, his magic had come easily. What was holding it back? Was it the Weers? Did the Weers have magic? No, it had to be something else—something within himself that was holding back the magic.

He had been overconfident before in his battles with the other monsters. Perhaps it was overconfidence that was holding his magic back, but he wasn't overconfident now. *Oh what is it?* he thought. Now he thought about Lela and Chalice. They had brought him here, the only boy in the whole of Ireland who could save Chalice. Only he had the power...

"Only I have the power!" he screamed suddenly. "I have it!" Instantly magic flared into his hand, blasting from him like a sky rocket. Zap! Zap! Zap! The blasts that burst from Eoin's hand tore right through the Weer's chest as it was about to rip out Drollo's throat.

Zap! Zap! Zap! Three more blasts finished the other Weers. The magic blasted into them, tearing and ripping, scattering their bodies into the trees. The fifth beast snarled when it saw the others were dead. It glared at Eoin. It was unafraid, and suddenly with a roar it leapt at him.

But magic instantly burst from Eoin's other hand and the wicked beast was blasted into tiny pieces and thrown back into the trees with the other dead Weers.

Pale-faced and dizzy, Drollo looked around. He could see all the Weers were dead. It was then he felt his shoulder and suddenly the thought of his injury horrified him. "Gando," he gasped. "I've been bitten. I've been bitten..." Tears ran down his face.

Eoin gaped at Drollo as he cried, "Kill me, Gando—quickly! Kill me now! I do not want to be like them. Kill me!"

Horrified, Eoin saw Gando raise his sword to kill Drollo. Just as Gando was about to kill Drollo, a blast of magic from Eoin spun the sword from his hand.

"What did you do that for?" shouted Gando, his face flushed with anger.

"I can't let you kill Drollo!" shouted Eoin. "Why? Why do you want to kill him?"

"Human Kind, I do not *want* to kill Drollo," said Gando quietly as he looked at the crying elf. "But I *have* to. Drollo has been bitten by a Weer. He will become one of them, and if he is allowed to live, he will hunt us, too. I do not want to kill him, but I must. If I had been bitten by a Weer, I'd want Drollo to kill me."

"Gando," pleaded Drollo. "Please. Do it now. Please you must. Don't let the transformation take place. Don't let...Ahhhhhhhh...Ahhhhhhhhh!"

Eoin gasped aloud when Gando pointed. Drollo's hands were already sprouting hair and his nails were growing longer even as they watched.

"Ahhhhhhhh!" screamed Drollo, writhing in terrible agony now as the bones in his face began to crack and grow longer. Now hairs were beginning to cluster on his brow and over his nose.

"I have to kill him now!" shouted Gando as Eoin gaped at Drollo's teeth. They were already protruding past his lips.

Picking up his sword Gando raised it again to kill Drollo.

⸎

"What are you going to do?" asked one of the oldest unicorns, whose name was Felic.

"What?" said Chalice, looking at him numbly. "There is nothing I can do—nothing."

"We all know you are the supreme one," said the old unicorn.

"How?" asked Chalice.

"We can see your magic," said Felic.

"My magic?" said Chalice.

"Yes."

Chalice looked around. All the unicorns were looking at him. Chalice could see their magic running up and down their horns.

"If the Weers do come for more of us, we must make sure you are kept to the last," said Felic.

"But Rashark will eventually find out who I am," said Chalice quietly. "The foul monster *will* take my magic. I will die sooner or later." He looked around again. "If only I had *more* magic I might be able to fight Rashark. If only my magic was more powerful..."

At this, old Felic snickered and his mane shook as he became very excited.

"If only I had all *your* magic, then maybe I would be strong enough to destroy Rashark and get us all out of here," said Chalice, tears glistening in his eyes.

Now the old unicorn became even more excited. "All *our* magic," he said thoughtfully. Then neighing loudly he rose up on his hind legs.

Just then several Weers appeared. Two of them began to whip at the unicorns who where near the edge of the herd.

"You'd better give up the supreme unicorn," snarled one of them. "And you'd better be quick about it, too, or our master will punish us."

Roaring with anger the two Weers began to lash out at the unicorns on the edge of the herd. Then four other Weers appeared and within a few seconds, twenty-five moaning unicorns were being herded out of the chamber. When they where gone, Felic pushed his way to the edge of the herd. He checked to make sure there were no Weers in sight. Then he quickly made his way back to Chalice. "Chalice," he whispered so as not to let the others hear him, "I have a plan that might prolong your life. It might save you long enough for your magic to grow stronger. It might help you escape from this terrible place."

The young unicorn stared at him. "A plan?" he exclaimed. "What do you mean? What plan could make my magic stronger?"

"Listen, as I explain to the others," said Felic. Then neighing loudly he began to push to the center of the herd.

CHAPTER TWELVE

The Ultimate Sacrifice

Felic now stood on his hind legs, and though he was neighing in a low voice, every unicorn heard it. "You all know Chalice is among us," he began.

Some of the younger unicorns voiced surprise. "Well he is," said Felic turning to Chalice. All the unicorns looked at Chalice as Felic continued. "You all know what will happen if the evil one takes the supreme Chalice's magic."

At this a low moan came from nearly all the unicorns.

"Yes," said Felic. "We will be no more. All unicorns will die if he perishes." Taking a deep breath, Felic went on. "You all know what it means to have your horn broken and your sacred magic stolen."

Several unicorns near him nodded. Others looked over at the unfortunate unicorns that had already had their magic stolen.

"What I am about to ask of you will be the supreme sacrifice," said Felic.

Chalice frowned, as did several older unicorns. Felic's next words caused an uproar among the beautiful creatures.

"I am asking you..." said Felic, his heart pounding. "I am asking you all to give up your sacred magic willingly."

The old unicorn's words were so shocking that it was several seconds before any unicorn spoke. Then the words, "Give! Give! Willingly! Willingly!" echoed around the chamber.

"Yes," neighed Felic. "I am asking you all to give your precious magic to the supreme Chalice—a supreme sacrifice for the supreme one."

There was a stunned silence that lasted for several seconds. All the unicorns were staring at Chalice as Felic now began to explain. "We are going to have our magic taken away from us, anyway. There is no escape from here. If we give our magic willingly to Chalice, then at least we have a chance to save him."

"Yes," said Felic, "we would be sacrificing our most precious possession, our magic. But we would be giving Chalice a chance to become powerful enough to destroy Rashark. We would be sacrificing ourselves, but we would be helping to save our brothers and sisters out in the land. If Chalice dies, they are doomed anyway. This way, we can make Chalice stronger." Turning, he looked at Chalice.

All the unicorns stared at Chalice. Then one of them shouted, "I will give *my* magic to Chalice!"

Then another shouted, "Me too!"

Soon the whole chamber echoed in agreement with Felic's plan.

Now Felic approached Chalice. "I will be the first to give you my magic," he said quietly.

Chalice, with tears still running down his face, bowed his head as Felic put the point of his horn against his. For two seconds magic fizzled between them at the point of each of their horns.

Chalice gave a snort as he felt the old unicorn's magic surge into him, and a second later it was all over. With a low moan, Felic turned and walked away through the herd; some of them moved quickly out of his way, as though afraid to touch him. Felic was not able to raise his head as he walked over towards the hornless unicorns that had no magic. He stood with them, looking down at the ground. His horn was as black as night now. His most precious possession—his magic—was gone.

With a heavy sigh and a low whinny, another old unicorn approached Chalice and touched horns with him. Slowly, Chalice began to get stronger and stronger.

❧❧❧

"No!" screamed Eoin. "Don't kill him! I'll use my magic!"

Gando turned to him. "No!" he shouted. "Don't use your magic!" Suddenly he swung his sword at Drollo. But before the blade could kill the unfortunate Drollo, Gando found he couldn't move. Eoin's magic was holding him rigid. His right hand was held out to Gando. The General tried to shout, but he couldn't.

Eoin placed his other hand on Drollo's shoulder. Immediately, both Eoin and Drollo were covered in a light so bright that Gando had to close his eyes. He did not see the force of Eoin's magic as it pumped into Drollo, who began to vibrate faster and faster. Suddenly

Drollo gave a piercing scream, and when Gando opened his eyes, he found he was able to move. Now he saw that Eoin had straightened and was examining Drollo. There was no sign of the Weer's bite on Drollo's shoulder. Grinning, he sat up.

Drollo was normal again.

Eoin began to sway and he felt himself grow faint. Gando reached out to grab him to keep him from falling. Concerned, Drollo rose to his feet and both elves studied Eoin.

"You fool!" cried Gando. "What have you done?"

"Done?" whispered Eoin, hardly able to talk. He felt so weak. "I've saved Drollo's life. He's okay now, isn't he?"

Gando spat angrily. "It would have been better to have killed him," he growled. "Do you not realize what you have done? Can you not feel it?"

"What? What have I done? I don't understand!" shouted Eoin, annoyed that the elves didn't seem to appreciate that he had saved Drollo.

"You've put too much of your magic into saving Drollo. Do you not feel how your power has diminished?"

Eoin frowned. He did feel weaker.

"Now you will not be strong enough to destroy Rashark. This has all been a waste of time—there is no use going on," exclaimed Gando, suddenly sitting down and burying his head in his hands. "It's all been a waste of time," he repeated sadly.

In fifty minutes nearly all the unicorns had given Chalice their magic, and he stood glowing with power as the last few waited for their turn. Five minutes later, when the last unicorn had given Chalice its magic, all the unicorns gathered around him.

Chalice stood in the middle of the herd, his horn now magically disguised and black like the others, and he was not glowing anymore. Even though they had given away their most valued possession, all the unicorns were strangely happy, and they began a pleasant hum.

The sound reached the ears of the Weers, and several seconds later about ten of them came into the chamber and began to whip at the herd. Then they noticed that all the unicorn's horns were black.

"What's happened?" snarled one of the biggest Weers.

"Their magic!" roared another. "It's gone!"

"We'll have to tell the master."

"You go!" shouted another Weer.

"I'm not going to tell Rashark anything," said one.

"Nor me."

"Who's going to tell the master?" shouted another Weer. "He'll have to know what's happened."

As they were arguing, the Weer that had been sent for the Seeker returned, and a few seconds later Rashark came roaring into the chamber. The monster saw at once that the unicorns had no magic. As a hundred of his Weers roared with anger and whipped at the herd to keep them in a tight circle, Rashark withdrew the Seeker from the folds of its cloak. Muttering black spells, the monster passed its hand over the Seeker that was in fact a glowing ball about the size of a tennis ball. "Seek," the monster whispered, and at once the ball floated from Rashark to the nearest unicorn. The Seeker hovered in front of the unicorn for a few seconds, then rose right up to its horn and moved closer to gently touch the point of its horn. Then it left that unicorn and danced to another, and then another.

"My Seeker will soon find out which of you has all the magic," boomed Rashark. "When it does, I will destroy Chalice, for there is no one else you would give up your miserable lives for!"

The unicorns whinnied. They were frightened for Chalice. Each watched as the glowing, dancing ball moved quickly from unicorn to unicorn. It would not be long before Chalice would be discovered. They could see now that though Chalice had powerful magic, he was not powerful enough to destroy Rashark. Now the Seeker began to dance towards the middle of the herd.

Chalice snickered silently and his heart was pounding as he saw the Seeker touch a unicorn a few meters from him, then jump to another. It would only be a few minutes before he was discovered. Then what would he do?

※

Eoin frowned. "What do you mean it's all been a waste of time? I still have plenty of magic. I can feel it. See?" he exclaimed, opening his hand and allowing a shaft of magic to rip from him and hit a huge tree. The thick trunk split right down the middle.

Gando shook his head. "Yes, you still have power-ful magic, Human Kind. But you don't seem to realize how much magic *Rashark* has. Even with your full power it was doubtful you could stand against him. But with much of your magic now gone..." He shook his head.

Drollo gaped at him. "Then we really are going back?"

Gando sighed. "I... I don't know what to do. To go on would be sure death for the Human Kind."

Drollo sighed. "I wish you had let me die," he said to Eoin.

"But—" Eoin frowned.

"It is done now," said Gando. "Come Human Kind. We will take you back." He moved to go, and Drollo followed. They had only gone a few steps into the trees when they realized that Eoin hadn't come with them. They returned to find him still sitting where they had left him.

"You said if this Rashark gets Chalice's magic, then he will destroy everyone in this land," said Eoin before they could even ask him why he was still sitting there.

"Yes," said Gando. "And other lands, too." Gando wondered what the boy was getting at.

"Even my land... Ireland?" asked Eoin.

Gando studied him. "Yes," he said quietly. "Even your Ireland. Rashark would eventually find his way there through the Warke. He would wipe out every Human Kind in Ireland."

"Then," said Eoin. "I'm going on. If you and Drollo won't go with me, I'll go alone." He stood up. "Now if you'll give me directions on how to get there..."

Gando looked at Drollo. Then smiling slowly he said to Eoin, "Are all your tribe as foolish as you are?"

"I hope not," said Eoin, half regretting he had said he wanted to go on. But he *did* want to go on. He was determined now to save Chalice or die in the attempt.

A few moments later the three were heading up out of the trees into the mountains.

At the same time the glowing Seeker was dancing from an old unicorn standing beside Chalice.

CHAPTER THIRTEEN

AN OLD ENEMY

AS THEY HEADED ALONG THE BRIGHTLY LIT PATH, Gando pointed at the two mountains a short distance away. The shadows of the mountains could easily be seen in the moonlight. Between the mountains was a narrow pass.

"When we go through yonder pass, there we must keep to the trees that grow on the far side. Rashark must not find out we are in his domain." *Not yet anyway*, he thought. He was still worried about Eoin's diminished power. He sighed silently. *At least this is better than returning to the Wiselfs and telling them we failed.*

He studied Eoin. *For a young Human Kind, he's brave*, he thought, trying to remember when he had been young. He had only been fifty years old when he had fought his first Weer. He had nearly died then. In the battle the Weer had torn his eye out, but he had slashed its face with magic rippling from his sword before escaping death by rolling down a cliff.

As they were making their way up the path, they were unaware that they were being followed.

As soon as the Seeker bounced onto Chalice's horn, all pretence was gone. Chalice and his horn immediately began to glow brighter and brighter. As he did, the Seeker suddenly shattered into a million pieces. Chalice's magic had destroyed it. Now the entire herd neighed with triumph and moved away from the supreme unicorn as his powerful magic sparkled all around him.

Rashark smiled when it saw Chalice. *At last*, thought the monster as it studied the power of Chalice's magic. *Soon I will have it all*. Rashark could see that the young unicorn's magic—though powerful—would not be powerful enough to defeat it. The thought of taking the young unicorn's magic made the monster's grotesque smile widen. Saliva ran in a steady stream down Rashark's chest as it thought about how it was going to enjoy playing with the young unicorn.

Rising on his hind legs and with his magic spluttering from his horn, Chalice showed how defiant he was. Though frightened, he believed he was strong enough to defeat the evil Rashark.

The other unicorns neighed loudly to encourage him.

Suddenly, a blast of pure magic, shot from Chalice's horn, hit Rashark just below its neck. The monster's eyes widened with shock when it felt the power of Chalice's blast. Caught unawares, it staggered back, but its own magic was quickly repairing the damage from Chalice's attack. Rashark would not be caught off-guard so easily again.

Chalice quickly sent a silent thought out to the herd. "*Gather around me.*" In the few seconds it took for Rashark to recover, the herd was pressing close around

Chalice—and he had disguised himself as one of them
again.

Roaring with anger, Rashark searched for the supreme
unicorn. All it could see was the herd of neighing, frightened unicorns. Without the Seeker, the monster knew it
had no way to tell which unicorn was Chalice. Still roaring, it blasted at the middle of the herd. Several unicorns
sank to the ground at once, their legs broken and useless.

Now the Weers moved in, whipping and roaring at
the frightened unicorns as Rashark sent two more waves
of magic into the herd. Twenty-three unicorns sank to
the ground, their legs broken, too. Rashark would have
killed them outright if it had not been afraid that Chalice would be killed as well.

Fearing for the herd now, Chalice pushed quickly to
the door of the chamber where around fifty Weers stood
whipping at the unicorns to keep them back. Another
two blasts of magic from Rashark's hands left thirty-one
unicorns lying on their backs. The monster's loud roaring echoed around the chamber, terrifying the herd and
sending them into a panic.

Suddenly, with a loud, shrill neigh and glowing all
over, Chalice exposed himself. Rising on his hind legs, he
let his magic rip into the Weers. A flashing beam of light
tore into the beasts guarding the door. As they fell dead,
Chalice screamed for the herd to follow him, and then
he raced out of the door.

All of this had happened in just a few seconds, but
Rashark and its beasts were caught unawares. With a
great bellow, the monster tore after Chalice, trampling
some of the herd on the way.

Chalice raced on, his magic pulsating through him. Soon he left the herd far behind, and glowing like a fiery ghost with his feet barely touching the ground, he raced towards the trees. *I must get to the garden*, he thought, glancing back through the darkness.

Suddenly his eyes widened with fear as he caught sight of Rashark, glowing much more brightly than he was—and the monster was catching up with him fast. Terrified, the young unicorn raced as fast as he could. He knew now that Rashark's magic was greater than his. He also knew that Rashark would catch him soon.

Eoin and the elves had reached the pass between the mountains. It was darker here, and Gando motioned them silently to stop. He moved right up to the entrance of the pass and peered up into the darkness. Sheer rock rose on both sides of the pass, which was about fifteen meters wide.

Drollo silently drew Gando's attention to Eoin's eyes. They were glowing brightly. The two elves knew that danger was nearby then, not only because of Eoin's glowing eyes, but because their ears had begun to wiggle.

"Be alert," whispered Gando as he led them into the pass.

As their eyes grew accustomed to the darkness, the elves soon discovered the source of their fear. There in the darkness in the middle of the pass, breathing as quietly as it could, stood a Weer that was ten meters tall. Its red, slanted eyes pierced the darkness, and they widened when Eoin and the elves came into view.

The first Eoin knew of it was when it gave a loud roar. The sound boomed from the walls of the pass and echoed all around them. It was then that Eoin saw the beast's red-veined eyes glaring down at them. Separating quickly, the elves withdrew their swords and allowed their magic to trickle onto the hilts.

Gando frowned as he stared up at the face of the Weer as it crouched and then tore at the air as it came towards them. The monster had a long scar across its face, which parted the thick, white hair that covered his skin. All at once, Gando recognized the Weer as the beast that had torn his eye out—and strangely enough, it seemed as though the beast recognized him as well.

The magic from my sword must have fused into it when I cut the Weer's face, thought Gando. *The magic must have kept working on the beast all these years to make him grow so big.*

"So it's the elf who gave me the magic when we fought," roared the Weer. "I took your eye then, elf— now I will take your other one before I tear you to pieces." Suddenly the beast gave a loud howl. The sound reverberated up and down the pass.

Gando gulped. He gulped again when he heard more howls behind him. Other Weers were entering the pass. They were trapped.

Once more, Eoin tried to call his magic. *Nothing! What's wrong?* he thought. *What stops it? It isn't overconfidence. No, I need it, just like Lela needs me. I need it to save Chalice. I need...needddddd...* Suddenly magic was flashing through and around the pass, lighting up the whole area. Opening the palm of his left hand, Eoin raised it in a halt sign in front of him. Four powerful blasts, one after the other, hit the giant Weer. Two ripped into its face and two hit it above its knees, and with an agonized roar it fell to the ground. As Eoin focused on the giant Weer in front of him, Gando and Drollo were facing the other two beasts that had come up behind them. Dancing nimbly around them, the two soldier elves cut and slashed at the Weers, keeping the beasts from getting near enough to tear at them.

Suddenly a voice spoke to Eoin inside his head, and the distraction almost gave the giant Weer an opening to grab him. But a quick blast from Eoin's hand hit it on one of its tearing claws.

"Eoin, you must finish the Weer quickly," the voice cried. "Hurry! Chalice is in great danger. Kill the Weer, then leave the elves and go. Save Chalice!"

⚜

As Chalice ran to escape Rashark, he came at last to the edge of trees that marked the pass. As he rounded a tall oak tree, he took another look behind himself. By then, Rashark was only about thirty meters away. But as Chalice glanced back, he failed to see a thick root that looped out of the ground at the bottom of the oak. With a shocked squeal, his front left hoof caught on the root and he tripped, rolling over and over to stop almost in the middle of the clearing.

Roaring triumphantly, Rashark raced around the tree towards Chalice, but a shimmering, protective dome of magic was covering the winded unicorn as he tried to scramble to his feet. It was the only thing keeping him safe as Rashark towered over him.

"Ha, ha, ha, ha, ha, ha!" laughed the monster. "Finally, supreme unicorn—you are caught. Ha, ha, ha, ha, ha, ha!" Rashark pointed down at Chalice to try and break through the protective globe with a barrage of magic. The force of the attack was so violent that Chalice had to push more and more of his own magic into it to make it stronger.

"Do you feel my power?" roared Rashark as it increased its barrage. "Feel it and wonder at how powerful I am. Soon I will take your magic, and then you will feel my even greater power. Ha, ha, ha, ha, ha, ha!"

Chalice neighed fearfully, but still grunting from the effort, he forced as much magic as he could summon into the vibrating globe to strengthen it. Still, he knew it wouldn't be long before Rashark would break through.

⁂

Zap! Zap! Two powerful blasts from Eoin's hands caught the Weer on the shoulders as it tried to scramble to its feet again.

"Finish it quickly!" the voice in Eoin's head screamed.

Suddenly another blast shot from Eoin's body and hit the giant Weer full on the chest. The incredible power of the blast made the Weer's eyes widen with shock, and its heart suddenly stopped. With a surprised look on its grotesque face it fell back and died.

Gando glanced quickly behind him at the sound of the blast, and Drollo smiled. Any moment now, the

Human Kind would turn to easily destroy the Weers that they were fighting. But out of the corner of his eye, Drollo saw Eoin leap over the giant Weer's body and race on up through the pass.

"Human Kind!" he screamed as one of the Weers took a swipe at him. Had he not ducked in time, it would have taken his head off.

Racing as hard as he could, Eoin didn't know where he was going, but his magic showed him. At the end of the pass to his left was a cluster of trees, and just beyond them he saw the intense glow of magic from Rashark and Chalice. Without hesitation, he headed in that direction.

The scene that confronted Eoin when he reached the clearing shocked him. He almost cried out with horror when he saw the towering monster, Rashark, as it tried to destroy the globe around Chalice. For a few seconds, Eoin didn't know what to do, but then before he could think, he shouted "Stop!"

For a moment, Rashark was distracted. It stopped its attack on Chalice and turned to see Eoin standing in the clearing. An evil smile spread across its horrible face as Rashark straightened to confront the intruder—and that smile terrified Eoin. But as soon as Rashark turned to face Eoin, Chalice rose silently to his feet. Still protected by his magic, but weakened by his massive use of it, Chalice slowly edged towards Eoin.

"You must be the Human Kind," said Rashark. Suddenly, the monster shot out a blast of magic that hit Eoin in the chest and threw him backwards. If Eoin's magic had not been bubbling through him, the blast would have killed him.

"Ha, ha, ha, ha, ha, ha, ha, ha," laughed the monster. "It seems that you don't possess as much magic as I was led to believe!"

But suddenly, Eoin shot a blast at the monster from where he lay on the ground, hitting it on the left arm so hard that Rashark spun around. He was facing Chalice again—who immediately blasted even more magic at Rashark.

With a surprised bellow, Rashark glared at the unicorn and boy. The monster was unhurt, though, and in an instant it had covered itself in a fine, protective shield of its own and then began blasting powerful black magic at them.

Eoin quickly scrambled to his feet to avoid the barrage, then he blasted back at the monster. Though still weak, Chalice was recovering rapidly, and a few seconds later he was strong enough to stand beside Eoin and send thumping blasts of magic from his horn straight at Rashark.

The monster's huge hands were a blur as they both blocked and shot magic back at the boy and the unicorn. It was strong enough to stand with its hands straight out, blasting a powerful barrage at both of them. But Eoin and Chalice, with their magic combined, had quickly, magically formed a thick, protective wall in front of themselves. The glowing wall moved slowly towards Rashark, but the monster summoned its greater magic to force it back.

As the battle continued, Rashark's smile widened. It was more powerful than the unicorn and the Human Kind—and Chalice and Eoin knew it as well. They knew it would only be a matter of time before the monster would overpower them.

∘❦∘

Meanwhile, the Weer that had leapt on Drollo suddenly jerked to a standstill as magic exploded into its back. With its hair singeing, it clutched in vain as it tried to reach its back, then fell dead almost on top of the elf. Drollo gaped at it, then he turned to see the second Weer stagger back as it roared its last breath.

Now the two elves stared at the one who had saved them.

"Dardo!" they cried out when they recognized the old Wiself.

"Yes," said Dardo. "But there's no time to explain. Come on! We have to help Eoin and Chalice. Already they are facing Rashark—and they are losing the battle. Come on!"

CHAPTER FOURTEEN

THE MEDAL

THE DISTANCE BETWEEN RASHARK, EOIN AND Chalice was about twenty meters. The magical wall flashed back and forth, back and forth, until suddenly Rashark forced it to a halt just three meters from the unicorn and the boy.

When the three elves reached the clearing, they were just in time to hear Rashark laugh as another burst of black magic pushed the wall another meter closer to Chalice and Eoin. The monster was winning. The elves studied Eoin and noted the bubbles of sweat on his pale brow. They could see he was weakening. And though magic still burst from Chalice's horn, his head was lowered. He, too, was weakening.

"Ahaaaaaaaaa!" roared the monster. "Soon I will have all the magic I need. Ha, ha, ha, ha, ha!"

Taking another deep breath, Rashark straightened its arms and sent another volley of magic straight at the wall. The blast tore a small hole in the wall and caught Eoin on the shoulder. With a surprised cry of pain, he was spun around and fell down heavily. As he hit the ground, the chain around his neck broke and his silver medal rolled onto the grass beside him.

"Ha, ha, ha, ha, ha. I am enjoying this!" roared Rashark.

Dazed, Eoin raised his head and was surprised to see Arthur race into the clearing. He gaped at the old Wiself in shock. Arthur was an elf. It was then he realized it had been Arthur's voice that had told him to get to the clearing and save Chalice.

Dardo and the others had arrived just in time, for Rashark was getting ready to overpower Chalice. A blast of magic from the old elf caught the monster full in the face.

Gando and Drollo stood helpless, as they saw Dardo, with magic spluttering from his hands, run to stand beside Chalice.

"You really think your magic will help, elf?" sneered Rashark.

But Dardo's magic was stronger than the monster realized. As the old elf raised one of his hands, a powerful bolt of magic hit the monster on the head, spinning it around. Drollo and Gando wondered where Dardo had acquired his powerful magic. They could only stare, mouths agape, as the battle began anew, and this time it was Dardo and Chalice who faced the monster.

Roaring with fury, Rashark continued to force his magic at Dardo and Chalice with one hand as it touched its head with the other. Instantly a band of protective magic encircled it. Now taking a mighty breath, the monster roared, "I will finish this now!"

At that instant it sent a shot of magic straight at the wall, shattering it. As Rashark's magic hit him, Dardo was flung back into the trees with a surprised cry, and Chalice dropped to his knees with a painful whinny. The monster had won.

"Ha, ha, ha, ha, ha, ha, ha!" laughed Rashark, "Now I will sample your magic, unicorn!"

Horrified, Eoin and the elves watched the monster reach for Chalice's horn to rip it from his head.

"No!" screamed Gando, and with his sword raised, he ran at Rashark, swiping into the surprised monster's leg and cutting a piece from it. With a surprised roar, Rashark half-turned and cuffed the elf General with one hand, sending him crashing back into the trees.

Using what little magic he had left, Chalice tried to stun the monster, but Rashark was too strong—and the feeble attempt only made it angrier. It reached again for Chalice's horn, but Drollo slipped behind Rashark and plunged his sword into the monster's lower back.

With another anguished roar, Rashark turned and reaching around, he pulled the sword from his back and threw it to the ground. He glared at Drollo, who stood there like a stone, terrified and helpless. Once again, Chalice tried to fight back and sent a flare of magic at the monster, hitting it on one leg. With a grunt, Rashark forgot about Drollo turned back towards Chalice.

"It's time!" it roared as it reached once more for Chalice's horn.

Eoin, who was still a little dazed, was staring at his medal. It was glowing brightly, and he was surprised to see a fizzle of magic spiral from his finger and bounce along the ground into it. Suddenly his medal began to change into a tiny, glowing silver ball. Eoin's eyes widened, but suddenly he knew what he had to do.

As he scrambled to his feet, he yelled at Rashark, "Let Chalice go!"

Rashark turned towards him, as it did, Eoin let it have it. The elastic on his sling-shot sang as it released the tiny silver ball. The next second seemed to pass in slow motion as the ball flew straight at the monster's chest. Rashark was still holding his hand out to break off Chalice's horn when the silver ball hit him right in the middle of his chest.

"Arrrrgggghhhhh!" he roared, his eyes widening with shock and pain.

Clutching his chest he staggered back, almost stepping on Drollo. The small hole the silver ball had made in the monster's chest was growing bigger and bigger, and everyone held their breath when they saw Rashark's magic—and all the magic the monster had taken from the unicorns—gush from the hole in its chest and roar into the sky. In flashes of brilliant light it separated and shot away to seek out its true owners like fireworks.

All the while Rashark roared in agony as the silver ball worked its way into the monster's black heart.

"Agggghhhhh!" Rashark gave a loud roar before suddenly stiffening. Then, with a low moan, the monster fell sideways and its huge body crashed into several trees, cracking three in half. Rashark was dead.

Drollo stared at the rapidly decomposing body of the most terrible monster who had ever lived for a moment, and then he remembered Gando. He ran into the trees and found him lying dazed—but alive—at the foot of a mossy tree trunk. A few seconds later, they both returned to the clearing and saw Eoin standing rigidly as if hypnotized. He was smiling, and Dardo was standing beside him. The elves knew everything was going to be alright; Rashark was dead and Chalice was saved.

It was then they realized Chalice had gone.

It didn't take long for Chalice to race back to Rashark's cave, and with their horns magically in place and their magic surging through them, all the unicorns herded the Weers back into the chamber. With the supreme unicorn leading them, the unicorns forced all the Weer beasts into the burning hole in the ground.

As soon as the last Weer was destroyed, Chalice led the herd out of Rashark's domain and headed towards Derrylyn village. On the way back, they passed Eoin and the three elves.

When they were back at the Council room, Dardo explained to everyone why he had gone into the Warke. "About two years ago, I was awakened by a strange dream. In the dream I saw the Oracle, and it told me that Eglin was in danger. The Oracle told me I had to enter the Warke and use up what magic I had to go to Ireland, where Eoin lived.

"The Oracle showed me what Eoin looked like, and where he lived. I was supposed to live in Ireland, build up my magic—and help pass some magic onto Eoin. The Oracle knew that Eoin would be brought to Eglin, and that any magic I could give to Eoin would be increased many times when he passed through the Warke. My own magic, too, would be increased. As you can see, I used most of what I had to heal myself." He felt his shoulder.

Trigon smiled. "We all thought when you disappeared into the Warke that you had gone mad or had been killed."

"I very nearly was."

Dardo turned to Eoin. "I hope you don't mind my deceit. But if I had told you that I was an elf from another land—six-hundred-fourteen years old—and that I wanted you to return with me and do battle with a monster the size of one of your buildings, I don't think you would have."

Eoin smiled. "I suppose not." Suddenly his eyes widened as he realized, "Then you really *are* six-hundred-fourteen years old?"

The old Wiself's eyes twinkled and he nodded as he stood up. "I think, Eoin, that it's time you returned to your own land. Come," he said to the others. "Let us escort our saviour to the Warke. Our magic will help to guide him safely home."

After Eoin had said goodbye to Lela and Chalice and the other cheering elves, he was escorted to the Warke. As they stood in front of the Warke, Eoin said to Dardo, "Will you visit me sometime?"

"I don't know if I can, Eoin," said the old Wiself.

"I'll... I'll miss you," said Eoin sadly.

"And I you," said Dardo, smiling.

Eoin looked into the swirling Warke, then asked, "Maybe you'll allow me to come back some day?"

Dardo looked at Trigon. Trigon shook his head.

"You wouldn't be able to stop me if I wanted to," said Eoin, holding up his forefinger.

Trigon shook his head again and smiled at Dardo. "That's true." He looked at the Warke. "But now I think you'd better enter the Warke. It's nearly morning. I believe you'll have some explaining to do when you return to the orphanage."

"Yes, I will." said Eoin.

Reaching out, Dardo shook his hand. "Eoin, I'll see you again someday," he whispered. "Now go."

Eoin stepped back towards the Warke. Already he could feel it suck at him. "Goodbye, Arthur," he whispered. There were tears in his eyes. Suddenly, he was in the Warke and swirling through it, his own magic and that of the elves guiding him back to Cloonalagh.

Moments later he was emerging from the Warke and found himself along the bank of the river Cloon, near the carrie. He shivered as he stared at the disappearing Warke, and when it was completely gone, he headed back to the orphanage.

The sun was rising on another new Irish day as Eoin walked along the road into Cloonalagh. He smiled as he saw blue magic flicker from the tip of his finger. *Who will believe the adventure I've had?* he thought as he walked. *I wonder... should I tell sister Attracta?*

But would Sister Attracta believe him? *No,* he thought sadly. *No one will believe me. But maybe I will go back through the Warke on my own some day. There must be other lands where I'm needed...*

With these sly thoughts, Eoin walked to the door of the orphanage as a bell rang.

ABOUT THE AUTHOR

Derry born writer Jack Scoltock has been writing for over thirty years. Now retired, he is able to write at his leisure. Before retirement, Jack ran a dive shop. He was a diver and was involved with the discovery of a Spanish Armada Galleon in Kinnego Bay, County Donegal, in 1971. His *Log Books*, which detail his joy of the discovery, can be seen as part of an exhibition on the Armada at the Tower Museum Londonderry. They were the start of his interest in writing about underwater discoveries.

Ireland—and particularly Derry—is the backdrop for many of Jack's stories. In his hands, magic and monsters become believable as his stories draw from his experiences. His many books are proof of his compelling and page-turning ability to keep most children reading his stories.

Jack still lives in Derry and has been married to Ursula for over forty years. He has two children and three grandchildren.

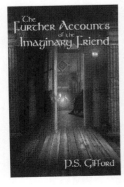

Also in Print from Virtual Tales